THE GOAT WITHOUT HORNS

THE GOAT WITHOUT HORNS

THOMAS BURNETT SWANN

WILDSIDE PRESS

*To Grover DeLuca,
great friend and guardian spirit*

Copyright © 1971 by Thomas Burnett Swann

A shorter version of this novel was serialized in *The Magazine of Fantasy & Science Fiction*, copyright © 1970 by Mercury Press, Inc.

Published by Wildside Press LLC.
www.wildsidebooks.com

ACKNOWLEDGMENTS

I wish to express a large debt to the authors of the following books: *Man and Dolphin*, by John C. Lilly, *Children of the Sea*, by Wilfred Bronson, and *A History of Everyday Things in England*, by Marjorie Quennell.

PUBLISHER'S INTRODUCTION TO THE SECOND EDITION

The following history—and it is a history and not a novel—contains events so incredible, so seemingly manufactured by an over-imaginative if not a downright melodramatic novelist, that the publisher feels called upon to remind the public of several significant facts:

First, that verbal communication was established with the dolphin, more specifically that species of dolphin known as *Tursiops truncatus,* within the last year. Sounds which for centuries had appeared to human ears no more than a series of squeaks and snorts from a playful animal were in truth a highly developed language with a syntax comparable to that of Japanese and a vocabulary as rich and often as confusing as Etruscan. Furthermore, the dolphin, that is, the brighter members of the species, had been understanding the conversation of men since the time of Aristotle and, with the good-humored tolerance of their race, waiting patiently for him to return the compliment.

Second, once communications was achieved, dolphins not only conversed with men but revealed what many marine biologists had long suspected, that they possessed a literature—oral, to be sure, since flippers and flukes do not lend themselves to wielding pens—as fluid in style as their own motions in the water.

Third, that this literature, which was passed from generation to generation by infinite repetitions, generally took the form not of epics, nor of plays, nor of poems, but of histories. One might expect so playful a race to write comedies crackling with epigrams in the manner of Oscar Wilde. Such was not the case. Except for two monumental histories, one of the entire dolphin race since their mass migration from the land to the sea forty-five million years ago, the other of the human race since men began to build boats, it was the custom of each dolphin clan to compose, singly or in concert, an account of an episode or episodes concerning their own particular history. The account was intimate and personal—not a broad record of the entire clan, written with the sweep and grandeur of a Gibbon—but events involving a few or perhaps a single individual, seen, recorded, and evaluated through the microscope rather than the telescope; microcosms, not macrocosms.

Fourth, when we presented such a history from the 1870s in our first edition last year, soberly labeling its nature on the cover and in our introduction, we were instantly accused of attempting to perpetrate yet another Gothic novel on a credulous public. Our Victorian dolphin narrator was variously identified with Mary Dewart, Victoria Bolt, and Daphne Duvalier. The ladies heatedly proclaimed that even if they had chosen to conceal their identities under pen-names (and why should such saleable names be concealed?), they would hardly have masqueraded as a fish, well, a mammal, but a fishy looking mammal all the same.

However, the authenticity of the book was attested by the renowned linguist, Julius Whipplejohn, who himself had anonymously transcribed the tale from the great-grandson of the dolphin narrator; and by author Thomas Burnett Swann, who had edited and attempted to clarify the roughnesses inevitable in a communication between a mammal that lived in the sea and spoke largely through his blowhole and a mammal that lived on the land and, assisted by tongue, teeth, and lips, spoke through his mouth. In a word, last year's "Gothic novel" is now widely recognized as a legitimate history of certain extraordinary events transpiring on a Caribbean island in the Nineteenth Century. Gothic perhaps in the sense of grotesque, macabre, inexplicable, but fully as historical as those larger grotesqueries, the Inquisition and the Salem witch hunts.

A word of caution. The island in question, though bearing superficial resemblances to both Tobago and Saba, has not been identified, and according to the great grandson of the narrator was totally submerged by the volcanic eruption of Soufriere in 1902.

CHAPTER ONE

I address my history not to my fellow dolphins, even though, following the custom of my race, I will repeat the words to my first son until he has learned them by rote and passed them in turn to his own first son. "My" history? "Charlie's history," I ought to say, for he is the subject and the hero, and it is to him and for him that I write, with the admiration of a warrior for a comrade-in-arms, and the adoration of one who swims but would like to walk, for one who walks like a god.

There was a time, earlier than our earliest recorded history, when dolphins lived on the shore, and walked on limbs which only later became flippers, and dwelled like rabbits in warrens or beavers in branch-built lodges. Our race eventually undertook a gradual migration into the sea, first becoming amphibians like frogs, then entirely sea-dwelling but still air-breathing. Perhaps our lives on shore had grown too difficult and too dangerous. Perhaps there were creatures which pierced our tender skin with giant claws or savage beaks, descended from trees to make a breakfast of us or emerged from the earth to drag us to their cackling young. Or perhaps we simply became restless and wished to explore a color different from green, a texture unlike dirt, a motion smoother than walking. For, as you know, we are the most adventurous of creatures, following the Gulf Stream north to Newfoundland every year and risking abrupt drops in temperature and bouts with sharks for the sheer joy of change, surprise, unpredictability.

I, for one, however, lamented my ancestors' decision to forsake the land for the damp, enveloping cleanliness of the sea. Now, if I could reconvert my flippers, I would instantly clamber back onto the shore and revel among the fields of cacao and the forests of mahogany, quite satisfied to walk or climb instead of swim. What did the sea ever bring me except the loss of my mother to a giant hammerhead? Men go into the sea to cleanse themselves of dirt, but how I would love to clamber ashore and roll on a sandy beach! My friends called me Gloomer because I would rather brood in a sea-cave than gambol and frolic like most of my light-hearted race.

Until the death of my mother, at least I managed an occasional somersault and a half-hearted nip of a shapely pubescent female.

But Mama saw through my pretence. "Son, you don't take after your family at all. As you well know, my lovers—and I have enjoyed more than any dolphin south of the Bahamas—call me Merry Mama, and your own dear father, the Great Triton rest his soul, could jolly a sea turtle out of a hundred-year gloom. Where have we failed you, dear?"

I deliberated. I was not one to make a quick answer. "You haven't failed me, Mama. I expect it's because I'm waiting."

"For a comely young cow?"

"I don't really know. Something. Someone. *A difference.*"

The first difference was the death of my mother, and I thought: This accounts for my gloom. The shadow of her death, like an inky cloud exuded by a squid, stretched backwards as well as forwards.

The second difference was Charlie.

Obviously I did not witness all of his adventures on the island of Oleandra, since many took place on the land instead of in the water. But Charlie told me much of what I could not see, and the rest I surmised—his thoughts, some of his actions, the facets of a character which seemed to me saintly and human at the same time. Though being as modest as he was lovable, he saw himself as rather an ordinary fellow and blamed himself for some of the horrors which overtook his friends. You see, the story is monstrous at times, as chilling as a confrontation with a tiger shark, as unlikely as an octopus or a narwhal, and the ending—well, you shall judge for yourselves.

While once or twice I may have erred (though not about Charlie's character), I think that my history on the whole is unevasive and accurate. I wish that parts of it—the horrors—were invented like the novels written by men, but dolphins are first of all historians. We have our anecdotes, and our tall tales, but our histories are strictest truth.

The shark which had killed my mother had not survived her, if that was any consolation. The leader of our herd, the Old Bull, had finished him with lethal blows to his underside, and afterwards the herd had been very solicitous of me. Not that I was a calf. I was five years old—in human terms, about eighteen. I was old enough to fend for myself, and when the herd skirted Oleandra, I decided to leave their company and linger near the little volcanic island which looked like an upright pinecone. My intuition—and a dolphin without intuition is like a man without reason—we call it our third ear—had not yet warned me.

They were greatly concerned at my decision. Dolphins are affectionate, familial creatures. Most of them are happiest in a herd. They considered my youth, my sorrow, and my inexperience, and they all but insisted that I follow the Gulf Stream north with them.

"Cape Hatteras. Do you want to miss all those big bouncing waves?" the Old Cow reproved me. She was probably an aunt, but considering the free morality of my race, it is sometimes difficult to establish family relationships. "Besides, your mother, bless her soul, would never forgive me if we left you here."

The Old Bull, a practical fellow of thirty ripe years, had the last word. It was worth heeding.

"Sharks. Too many around the island. Must be something in the water they like to eat."

"Well," I said gloomily, "now there will be two somethings. I would make a tasty morsel for a hammerhead."

"Indeed you would," said the Old Cow. "You've been gorging yourself out of grief."

"I may be plump," I pouted, "and irresistible to hammerheads. But I'm still staying. Give me a little more length and a little less girth, and let the sharks beware!" Suppose I battled and lost; what had I to lose except my life and my gloom?

When the herd reluctantly left me to my whims, I drifted, grieved, and ate, catching unwary mullets by the thousand because I felt less alone when my four stomachs were occupied; following a ship for a few miles out of habit without even noticing if the sailors were waving and throwing me fish.

Oleandra was a curious island: a big volcanic cone, long since dead, its outer slopes sere from the beating of winds or gnarled with stunted, twisted sea grapes, its protected crater lush with oleanders and frangipani and cupping a lagoon as green as a mermaid's hair. The Old Bull had shown me an underground passage which led from the sea into the lagoon.

"If the sharks get too troublesome," he had said, "you can always nip into the lagoon and hope they won't follow your scent. The entrance from the sea is hidden by rocks, and sharks, remember, have notoriously bad eyes."

The days passed, perhaps a week, perhaps a month, with no dimming of sorrow and no sharpening of any appetite except for food. And then, in the mist of days, I saw a ship, and time resumed for me...

She had anchored a few hundred yards from the shore, and she was not one of those island-hopping schooners with barnacled hulls and crusty captains. She was a schooner, it is true, but bright and red and slim of line, with sails as gossamer as the wings of a flying fish. Swaying in the turbulence, she seemed to have alighted unwillingly from the sky and to contemplate a quick return. She belonged to Elizabeth Meynell, the English lady who owned the island and lived in a large red house inside the crater. Once a month, the Old Bull had said, this schooner brought her mail and supplies from Martinique.

There was no dock or jetty. The waters which ringed the island, always choppy, were often so turbulent that anything built by man would dissolve into foam. There was neither a beach nor a harbor, but a tiny cove where Carib Indians were lowering a dugout canoe from a low shelf of rock and pushing off from shore. The paddlers—three Caribs with black slits in their cheeks and countenances to match their barbarous adornments—paddled rapidly if sullenly out to the schooner and, on the leeward side, attached their canoe to the larger vessel by ropes like a shark sucker to a shark. A single passenger swayed his tortuous way down a rope ladder and prepared to step into the dugout.

It was my first sight of Charlie.

A dolphin on the surface of the water can see with perfect clarity anything in front of him, beside him, or under him, but because of the position of his eyes it is difficult for him to see anything higher than sixteen or seventeen feet above him—a high-flying seagull, for example—without actually leaping into the air. I could not see the top of the schooner's mast. But I could see the deck and the passenger as he began to descend the ladder. I might have thought him a sailor lad from his brawny hands and his stocky frame. But his face—well, it was downright archangelic. Not angelic. Not simpering and pallidly virtuous, nor suggestive of harps and gossamer, but strong and kind and I suspected, capable of a martial fire when directed from the heavens. In a word, a young Gabriel or Michael.

My immediate reaction needs some defending. Perhaps, being a male, even though delphinese, I was instinctively jealous of his looks, just as human males resent a man who is too handsome. Perhaps I had been so gloomy and petulant for so long that I needed to work some mischief. Perhaps—indeed, probably—I was listening to my third ear and I hoped instinctively to frighten him away from Oleandra for both of our sakes because I sensed that he was somehow sacrificial, and I was soon to become inseparable from his fate.

At any rate, I gave the canoe a forward nudge and Charlie dropped not into it but beside it into the water. Then I surprised myself by a piece of sheerest perfidy. I skulked under the surface and nudged him as if I were a shark foraging for dinner. In the murky waters it was hard for him to recognize me as a relatively small dolphin. But he did not panic; somewhere, he had learned that under shark attack you try to remain calm, you never flail and hit and kick like a drowning man. With quick, deliberate movements, getting, by the way, no help from the Caribs, he seized the gunwale and simultaneously hoisted and rolled himself into the canoe. Only then did he peer into the water to see what kind of attacker he had escaped. When he spied a four-foot adolescent dolphin instead of a twelve-foot tiger shark, he began to laugh. He was not angry; he was not embarrassed; he was amused, and not with me but with himself. It was a laugh of self-deprecation, amiable and infectious.

I circled the boat, feeling and trying to look remorseful but knowing that most men cannot read our expressions, all of which they generally mistake for a grin. Charlie, oblivious to his dripping clothes, was watching my antics with continued good humor. But when the Caribs pushed off from the schooner, someone called to him from the deck. It was the captain, a bearded, square-set bear of man with a gruffness which was really kindness.

"Charlie boy, I give you one month on that island and you'll be swimming to meet us! Remember, we sail from Martinique the first of every month with mail and supplies."

Charlie. So that was his name. It was right for him. Charles would have been too formal. Charlie, unlike Billy, a sailor's name, sounded young and friendly and just nautical enough for someone who had sailed the Atlantic without actually being a sailor.

"I've signed on for a year," Charlie said, "and a year it'll be."

"You haven't met the young lady yet," said the captain, faintly greeted by a snicker from some of the crew. "Your—er—pupil, did her mother say? She usually comes with the Caribs to meet us."

But the Caribs had no intention of pausing for conversation. They had not greeted the passenger nor offered to help him when he fell into the water. Now, they ignored his presence in their boat and rowed as if his ship were carrying rats infected with bubonic plague.

Charlie raised his hand in a last, decisive goodbye, a year's good-bye, and then he looked at me, breaking into a grin when he saw me still frantically circling the boat to attract his attention and, yes, to stare at him.

He was a youth about my own age (in human terms, that is, eighteen or nineteen). His hair was the yellowest I had ever seen, yellow as the shower-of-gold tree, and the wind had tossed and tangled it into a silken tumult. But he was not, on the whole (thank the Great Triton), ethereal. His face was ruddy and healthy and English, and his stalwart frame, middling in height, planted him firmly on earth and within range of friendly overtures from an unethereal dolphin.

Looking up from me, he examined the island which was now within a hundred yards. He tried to look excited; he tried to look anticipatory, as if remarkable adventures awaited him. But a sadness darkened his face. No, "darkened" is hardly accurate. Charlie's gold was without shadows. "Suffused" is the proper word, with its hint of light even in sadness. It was not a face which was meant to be sad. The contours were shaped by the configurations of joy. But something had happened to him very recently. He was not so much coming somewhere as he was leaving somewhere, and forgetting—or trying to forget—a lost, loved person. I knew then that we were destined to become friends. We were divided by the barrier which separates the sea from the shore, but linked by a kindred loss

THE GOAT WITHOUT HORNS | 17

and a kindred need. I swam behind the canoe almost until it was beached (or rather, lifted out of the water by waiting Caribs, since as I have said there was no beach).

After Charlie had tried to drop into the canoe and dropped by mistake into the water, his luggage and Mrs. Meynell's mail had been lowered with more success into the canoe. With much grunting and scowling the Caribs now proceeded to strap a small trunk and a carton brimming with books onto the backs of two burros, which would carry them up the precipitous wall of the crater, over the top, and down to the Red House inside the crater.

I did not want to see the last of Charlie. I felt cheated; indeed, I felt outraged, and cursed the Great Triton under my breath. My punishment was prompt. One of the Caribs began to pelt me with stones. Of course he missed; the reactions of a dolphin, even a plump dolphin, are instantaneous. I ducked agilely under the water and out of range. But Charlie saw the action. He did not hit the man; he did something much more demeaning to the man's pride. He gave him a prompt, powerful shove and the Carib, though taller by a foot and pounds heavier, landed on his back. When he scrambled to his feet, Charlie repeated his shove without bloodying his fists and without once being touched by the Carib's flailing hands. This time the man's friends restrained him with the gibberish, part original Carib, part African, and part English, which passes for their language. It is a gibberish which I have tried to learn, but I sensed that the man was being counseled to bide his time (the English phrase "Goat without horns" appeared several times) while Charlie stood his ground like a boy fresh from Eton at the Battle of Waterloo.

He gazed back at me and raised his hand in a gesture of farewell. I leaped out of the water and spun in the air. Men always expect us to perform antics, however melancholy we may feel, and if I had to frolic to hold his attention, I would turn a triple somersault. He called after the Caribs to wait for him. They glowered and halted the burros. Charlie was not to be hurried. I eased so close to the bank that I scraped my skin on a projecting root, but I gave no thought to the scrape when Charlie, with beautiful courtliness, leaned over the water, touched my head, and allowed his fingers to linger as if to say, "There is no strangeness in your wet, dark skin to me." He was communicating in the only way possible at that time. After all, what else does one do with a dolphin when one does not understand his language? Shake his flipper? I said good-bye. To Charlie the words must have seemed a raucous squeak, but he guessed my intention.

"You can't understand me," he said (and I understood every word!), "but I think we will meet again. Good friends are not to be parted for long."

The Caribs, needless to say, had not waited for him; they were driving the burros up the slope and strewing Charlie's books behind them. With a decidedly unethereal oath, he gathered the books and overtook the strewers, who stopped beating the burros. Until they had left the range of my vision, I watched them ascend that windblown, tree-gnarled slope where clinging was a part of climbing.

Then I set out to find the opening which led into the lagoon.

CHAPTER TWO

Now I must tell you about Charlie, about him before he came to Oleandra and why he came; about the grief which sent him wandering to the islands instead of continuing at Cambridge. Historians are allowed to digress about their heroes and villains, and my digression, as you will see, helps to explain why I made him the hero of my history. You may wonder how I, a dolphin, presume to speak knowledgeably about an England and a queen I have never seen and an age which I have viewed only from the sea. My teacher in such matters, my collaborating historian, was Charlie. Our methods of collaboration were unconventional since, for a long time, Charlie was unaware that I understood and remembered his English, and remembered it with the clarity and exactitude of a race whose literature is oral instead of written.

Charlie was a boy who, expressly created to love, found himself suddenly bereft of love. He did not remember his father, a civil servant in India who had died when Charlie and his twin brother Kenneth were infants in London, but his mother was parent, guardian, and goddess, and he never thought to lament the lack of a father. When she sent her sons to Marlborough at the age of twelve, it was not to be rid of them but to educate them, and they hurried to rejoin her in London for every holiday including that cornucopia of holidays, the summer. In short, she was a mother who would have liked to dote but who forced herself, for the good of her sons, to appear merely warm, loving, and affectionate; and she was blessed by sons who judged all other women by her standards, her grace, courtesy, and most of all compassion, and could not find her equal.

Charlie was a light-hearted boy, because sadness must be learned, and for nineteen years he had no teachers. Then, he was taught supremely well. After Marlborough he and Kenneth had completed a year at Cambridge. Charlie had gone to spend a summer weekend with a friend at Chichester. He was summoned by messenger to London, where he learned that both his mother and his brother had contracted typhoid fever, the same disease which had killed the Prince Consort and driven Victoria into a decade of mourning.

They died the next day and Charlie was inconsolable. He could not foresee an end to his grief; he did not want to die, but he did not want to live. He could not escape his own identity, his own remembrances, but at least he could escape his country and the places where he most remembered his mother and Kenneth. He decided to travel. He stood heir to a moderate fortune; in other words, he possessed the means to leave England. He approached his mother's solicitor, the man who would handle his estate until he came of age, and received the assurance of a generous allowance which would allow him to travel as far as he chose and to any country of his choice. Since his object was forgetfulness and not pleasure, he must choose with discretion. Should he tour Europe like Lord Byron, whose poetry he adored (though it was out of fashion with most Victorians), whose womanizing he accepted without judgment, but whose posturing he disliked? No, there was something theatrical in a Byronic grand tour at such a time, particularly if one recorded one's grief in four best-selling cantos. Should he take service in India like his father? The remoteness would have pleased him but the associations, even though he had never known his father, would have proved intolerable.

Two months, one day, and eleven hours after the death of his mother and Kenneth, he saw an advertisement in the London Times which promised distance and change and a measure of welcome challenge:

"*Wanted:* A young man between the ages of twenty and twenty-five, of genteel connections, presentable appearance, and classical education. Cambridge or Oxford preferred. *Duties:* To tutor the daughter of Mrs. Elizabeth Meynell of the Red House, Oleandra Island, British West Indies. Interested parties please consult Mrs. Meynell's solicitor, James Long of Long, Snedley, and Barrows, 23 Grosvenor Park, between the hours of nine and eleven on Tuesday, November 3."

A reader of Gothic novels might have found presentiments of doom in a name like the Red House—blood, plagues, Poe's "Masque of the Red Death"—but Charlie, though his Celtic fancy did in fact possess a Gothic strain, thought at once of the poet and painter William Morris, who had built a medieval manor house by that name and had been imitated in England and, apparently, as far as the West Indies.

He arrived at eight-thirty and found himself already preceded by a dozen young men in various stages of confidence, impatience, and anxiety. He was greeted by a woman of indeterminate years, fixed smile, and skin so huge and flaring that Charlie expected her to float out of the window like a hot-air balloon. She took his name ("Mr. Lane will find out everything else"), and directed him to an over-stuffed chair which was trimmed with red silk tassels. Feeling altogether swallowed by the chair, which was large enough to hold Queen Victoria and most of her children at the same time, he awaited his turn with the impatience of one to whom inactivity had become a torment. There had been a time when he could enjoy equally a cricket match or an hour of contemplation under an alder tree, But now to contemplate meant to remember, and he sometimes found tears running down his cheeks when he was riding a train or shaving in front of the mirror which he had once shared with Kenneth. When he could not act, when outward inactivity was forced upon him as now, he activated his imagination and replaced, if he could, the spectres of grief with the phantoms of fancy. The chair, he decided, was a man-eating plant. There was no question that he was sinking deeper into its—stomach, should one say?—and that its digestive juices would soon begin to disintegrate him.

He had a long wait. Apparently each young man was questioned at great length, and Charlie began to despair of winning a position for which one must be examined as if one were sitting for a fellowship at Cambridge. But one by one his predecessors filed from the office, and not a single expression radiated victory.

After the first boy emerged, Charlie turned his attention from man-eating plants to possible reasons for rejection. This boy was patently a dullard. No one with such vacant eyes—erased blue was the best description—could teach a young girl anything but croquet. This boy was an egotist. Charlie had seen him enter with the swagger of assured triumph; he now looked like a defeated gamecock. Even his hair seemed crestfallen. But soon he would be boasting to his friends that the position had been beneath him. This boy looked too sickly to survive a voyage to any Indies, even the reasonably accessible Western ones. This boy was, to put it bluntly, unorthodox in looks. Did he lack what the advertisement had termed "presentable appearance"? He was neatly dressed, he was courteous and soft-spoken when he took leave of the fixedly-smiling secretary. He looked intelligent, he was certainly a gentleman, and the girl he tutored would not embarrass her mother by getting a crush on him. But his outsized nose looked like a carrot and his ears turned over at the tips like wilting lettuces. In short, he resembled an ambulatory vegetable garden.

In fact, Charlie noticed that several boys appeared to have been rejected because they lacked presentability. Was he himself presentable? He and Kenneth, identical twins, had decided that they were not tall enough to cut a dashing figure in the world of society, and they had used this presumed deficiency to evade invitations garnered for them by their mother. Otherwise, looks had not concerned them. Mirrors, it seemed to Charlie, were for shaving and not preening. True, he had sometimes been complimented by young ladies on his "Byronic nose" and his "hair like daffodils." But at nineteen his experience with the opposite sex was limited; and who could trust the fulsome compliments of those simpletons with whom he waltzed and whom through his mother's urging and in the company of their own mothers, he called on in their salons and gardens?

At last his turn had come. The secretary nodded toward a door whose heavy oak paneling looked about as inviting as that to the office of the headmaster at Marlborough, whose favorite adage had been, "Cane a boy once a month. It's as necessary as exercise and sound diet."

When Charlie entered the room, he felt a return of confidence. It suffered from an excess not of austerity but of opulence. Following the general taste of the day, and ignoring the salutary influence of John Ruskin and William Morris, the walls were crowded with gilt-framed pictures, a Gainsborough here, a Reynolds there, and elsewhere a host of stiffly posed family portraits. He had to weave his way among rosewood tables, which he momentarily expected to collapse under such bric-a-brac as wax flowers beneath glass, cuckoo clocks, and candlesticks. Still, for its style, it seemed both expensive and respectable; Mr. Lane was known to represent some of the oldest families in London.

The solicitor wheezed an unintelligible hello (or was he simply coughing?) and proceeded to look him up and down with embarrassing intensity, and to make notes, unconsciously muttering the words that he recorded in a small book with covers of tooled leather.

"Height—middling." Such a lacklustre adjective! A simple "tall" would have resounded with dignity; even a nondescript "medium" would have been acceptable.

"Build—sturdy. Good at wrestling, I should say."

Charlie was poised to admit that he did indeed like to wrestle when he remembered that Mr. Lane was not asking a question and in fact was probably not aware of his own muttering.

"Face—handsome but manly. Not in the least effeminate. Not one of your pretty boys."

Handsome indeed! That was a revelation, though Charlie did not particularly care, unless his face helped him to get the position, which was growing more attractive the more difficult it seemed of attainment.

"Now sit down, my young friend. Relax and we'll have a little chat." Mr. Lane, it appeared, had not been rude when examining Charlie like a hog at a county fair. He had simply been following the instructions of his client.

"Let me explain the situation. The advertisement in the *Times* was cryptic, to say the least. Mrs. Meynell worded it, by the way. To put it bluntly, she is a lady of enormous wealth and occasional eccentricities who some years ago lost her husband while cruising through the Indies on their yacht. She did not choose to return to England. She chose to bring England to her. She bought an island—an entire island, which she renamed Oleandra—it had been called Shark Island by the natives. She imported overseers and materials from London, and built a house on the style of William Morris. His Red House, don't you know. You *do* know, don't you?"

"Yes, Mr. Lane. I went to Marlborough."

"A fellow alumnus. I'll wager they remember Morris well at his old school. At any rate she was left with an infant girl who is now at an age when her mother wishes her to be tutored in subjects which in my own youth—and Mrs. Meynell's, I might add, she's a lady of some forty-five or fifty years—were thought unsuitable for young ladies, and rightly so. Some of these new fangled sciences. Bad enough for a boy, but Mrs. Meynell insists on them for her daughter. Geology. And biology. Can you imagine? *With emphasis on marine life.* Mrs. Meynell's own words. And that far-fetched nonsense about the apes. Evolution. I don't even like to say the word. It makes one feel so—simian. I trust you finished your studies at Cambridge or Oxford?"

A lesser school, it seemed, was beyond consideration.

Charlie spoke staunchly, though with a sinking, no, a sunken heart. "I've only had one year at Cambridge. You see, I'm not quite twenty." The advertisement had implied a degree and expressly stipulated an age. Sheer presumption had brought Charlie to the interview, and now, at the moment of reckoning, he refused to be cowed.

The silence was broken only by the ticking of three cuckoo clocks which showed the hour to be variously 11:15, 11:25, and 11:31. Charlie held his ground, or rather his chair, but he felt that if one of the clocks cuckooed he would start from the room like a flushed stag.

"How close to twenty?"

"Eleven months and one week."

"A bit of a gap, but we might stretch a point there. It's the education Mrs. Meynell is really concerned about. You weren't, I take it, expelled?"

"No. My grades were more than satisfactory. I won the Chancellor's Medal for the best poem, in fact." It was an annual college honor in which Tennyson as an undergraduate at Cambridge had long ago anticipated Charlie with a very bad poem. "It's just that I—I lost my mother, and also my brother who was with me in school, and I want to leave Cambridge for awhile. Come back and finish in a few years, perhaps. But not now."

Mr. Lane patted Charlie on the shoulder. One would not have thought him capable of such tenderness. There must be tears streaming down my cheeks, thought Charlie, longing for a chance to mop surreptitiously with a handkerchief. "I understand, my boy, I understand. But we mustn't stint Mrs. Meynell and her daughter, must we? If she wants biology with emphasis on marine life we must give her sharks and dolphins and cuttlefish, mustn't we? Are you scientifically inclined?"

"I studied geology at Marlborough. We made a lot of field trips. All those rolling downs make good digging. And you learn some archaeology along with the geology. But biology—I've always liked the sea and what's in it, but I'm not learned in the subject. I can learn, however. I can read on the voyage to Oleandra."

"Personally," muttered the barrister, "I don't know what good biology or geology will do a young girl in the first place. In my father's youth, he was taught that the world was formed in the year 4004 B.C., followed in a few days or years, depending on how long you reckon a Biblical day, by Adam and Eve. And that was that. Things are so much more complicated since we've begun to question the Scriptures. At any rate I think we can pass you in the sciences. Now then. We come to the most important subject of all. Mrs. Meynell particularly emphasized poetry. 'Don't send me a young man who calls Wordsworth Wadsworth,' she cautioned me. Seems she has an inordinate love for the stuff—er, art. You say you write it, but do you know the Masters? Suppose we give you a little test. Incidentally, she devised it herself. Not much for poetry myself. Passing it is one of her conditions, though, and every one of the young men ahead of you failed it. That is, except for the chap with the big nose. But he had other disqualifications. We'll do it this way. I'll quote a line and then you'll quote the next line and tell me the title and the author. Sounds hard, eh?"

If he quotes Wordsworth, I'm doomed, thought Charlie.

"Shall I compare thee to a summer's day..."

Good. An easy one. "Shakespeare. Sonnet XVIII. The next lines are:

'Thou art more lovely and more temperate.
Rough winds do shake the darling buds of May
And summer's lease hath all too short a date...'"

Charlie was prepared to complete the sonnet, but Mr. Lane grew visibly impatient and interrupted him.

"Splendid, my boy, splendid. Most unusual to find a knowledge of poetry in a sturdy chap like you. Built like an athlete. Played cricket at Marlborough, I'll wager."

Yes, he admitted. And Rugby and soccer, and he had wrestled and boxed and swum in water cold enough to frostnip a penguin.

"And yet you know your poetry. I guess you take after young John Keats. All that rot about Truth and Beauty, but he knew how to handle his fists. And Lord Byron, they say, was no slouch with a sword. Let's try one more:

'The child is father to the man.'"

Charlie shuddered. It was Wordsworth, but fortunately not difficult Wordsworth.

"Don't know that one, eh?"

"Oh yes. I missed it once on a test and looked it up later. The title is the first line. *'My Heart Leaps up When I Behold.'* And the lines after the ones you quoted go:

*'And I could wish my days to be
Bound each to each by natural piety.'*"

Mr. Lane sighed with the relief of one who had himself passed a difficult examination. "Young man, if you want the job, it's yours. As you know, the pay is lucrative. Oleandra is said to be one of the loveliest islands in the West Indies, and Mrs. Meynell, for all her eccentricities, is a damned fine-looking woman. Opulent, one could say. Lots of everything but nothing in excess. Not one of your starved Pre-Raphaelite beauties. Of course I haven't seen her in sixteen years. The tropic sun may have ruined her complexion, or she may have run to fat. I repeat, if you want the job it's yours. But consider carefully. It's a long way from home."

"I haven't any home anymore. My mother's solicitor has put the London house up for sale."

"No home? Nonsense. You still have Cambridge. Why not go back and finish your studies? A cricketer *and* a poet. What a combination! After that, you'll be looking for a wife, and a lucky girl she'll be, if I may say so. You're not to think of marrying one of those island women. Mrs. Meynell is too old and her daughter is too young, and most of the native population is indian. Caribs, they're called, not India indians."

There was something both touching and paternal—and also disquieting—in the old man as he cautioned Charlie about the job he had just offered him. In loyalty to his employer, he had praised the job; but his reservations were all too evident.

"I'll come back and finish at Cambridge one day, I hope, but not now."

"Let me come straight to the point. As I say, I haven't seen Mrs. Meynell since she lost her husband. She pays me a sizeable fee. I follow her instructions to the letter. But sometimes I wonder if—well, grief might have softened her brain."

"How do you mean, Mr. Lane?"

"The things she has me order for her. Weapons of all kinds. Swords from India. Nooses used for strangling by that infamous sect, the Assassins. Cannons of every make. It's as if she were collecting for a man's trophy room."

Except for her choice of Wordsworth, Mrs. Meynell had impressed Charlie as an extraordinary woman. Now he came to her defense. "Don't you think it's her way of revering her husband's memory? Adding to his collection, I mean? The Queen, they say, has a fresh suit of clothes laid out for Albert every day, and he's been dead as long as Mr. Meynell." He could understand such observances. He treasured his shaving mirror as if it were cut from diamond because his brother had shared it with him.

"Mrs. Meynell's husband did not collect weapons. He collected wines and liquors—whenever he could resist guzzling them. Bibulous Bobby, we used to call him. But I've said more than I should. If you've made up your mind, you must go ahead with a stout heart and a strong back, as we used to say at Eton. Mrs. Meynell may be mad as a hatter, but she will be good company, you may be sure of that. For all I know, she wants you for herself instead of her daughter." He hastened to clarify. "To quote poetry, I mean. You can be David to her Saul, if you'll forgive my likening an English lady to a Jewish king. She includes a line or two in every letter she writes me. For some reason, the last one stuck in my mind. Couldn't make head or tail of it:

'Childe Roland to the dark tower came."

"Browning."
"Mrs. Browning, eh? Now there was a great lady."
"Robert, I mean."
"Oh, the obscure one. The Sordello fellow."

And so Childe Roland had come to Oleandra.

CHAPTER THREE

Charlie's first impression of Oleandra was that he had accomplished his purpose: that he had substituted the alien for the familiar, the exotically memorable for the wistfully remembered. That monumental leech called grief, which feeds on memories, would not be starved by a change of landscape, but at least it would not be fed by a house in London or the downs of Marlborough.

Certainly the burros, the Caribs, the circuitous climb up the side of the crater, over the rim, and down through frangipani and mountain immortelle, kapok and shower-of-gold, was totally alien to him. Outside the crater, the winds had screeched and whistled and beaten the sea grapes against the disheveled earth; inside the crater, the riot of birds and flowers, the intensity of colors, had seemed not even remotely English; a jungle instead of a forest, with red-bellied trogons and rufous-tailed jacamars, whose very names, laboriously learned from *Birds of the Indies* by Father Jeremiah McIntosh, immediately distinguished them from the larks and blackbirds of home.

But then there had been the quieting of the winds as they descended the inner slopes and a little pleasant lane of stone cottages with thatched roofs and, substituting admirably for hollyhocks and geraniums, neatly trimmed hedges of crimson bougainvillea. He felt a curious revulsion, even a sense of betrayal. What right had an English village to twinkle on the inner slopes of a crater in the West Indies? One of the cottages, it was true, was reached by a path which ran between two enormous cannons. Still, they were English cannons, rusty, innocuous, looking as if they had come from a museum in the suburbs of London. Why could they not have been Spanish or Moorish or Malay or anything strange and alien and yes, sinister? (He was later to learn that the master of the cottage was not to be judged by his cannons.)

At the end of the village the path curved sharply into a small forest of oleanders, some of them growing to ten or more feet and spreading their tapered leaves into graceful green fingers which flaunted an abundance of pink and white flowers like so many rings. Another curve of the path and he saw the Red House, and he was inescapably back in England, looking at the house which Morris had built for his beloved bride, Jane Burden, in 1860. Here in painstaking imitation—and many a pain had been taken to transport the bricks from England—was the tranquil and restrained Gothic beloved by Morris; Gothic in its purity and simplicity rather than its grotesquerie. Here was no Castle of Otranto; here were no black, bristling turrets and waterspouts ending in gargoyles, but a warm expanse of red brick, a high-pitched red-tiled roof, and three gables, each with tall sash windows through which no Duke of Otranto ever seemed to have peered; furthermore, the trees which randomly sprinkled the lawn were not funereal yews or moss-laden oaks but apple blossom cassias, abloom with clusters of pink-white flowers and deep pink buds.

His disappointment was acute. He had crossed the Atlantic and half of the Caribbean to escape England, to renounce England, to forget England, and here was the very country of his grief resurrected in miniature and, what was worse, in its milder aspects. After talking with Mr. Lane, he had, like the heroine of Northanger Abbey, anticipated something not only different, but barbarous and even threatening. His landing with the Caribs had been an adventure, the ascent of the crater like a journey up a lunar mountain. He had been stirred, troubled, angered, frightened until, for the moment, he had forgotten his grief. But the tranquilities of the Red House seemed precisely calculated to recall his mother, whom he had always associated with green gardens and gracious houses. It was if he were coming home but only in a dream which he knew to be a cruel deception. Where were the eccentricities with which Mrs. Meynell had startled the staid Mr. Lane?

In sight of their mistress' house, the Caribs dropped their gloom and petulance; they chattered merrily; they vied to unload Charlie's baggage; they began to address him, in their polyglot language, with a word which was unmistakably "master." At first he supposed that they wanted a gratuity and wondered if they would accept English pounds.

Then be saw the reason for their transformation. Mrs. Meynell was standing in the arch of the main door. Mr. Lane had thought her a splendid and opulent woman. *Sixteen years ago.* She still looked exactly as the barrister had pictured her: "Lots of everything in exactly the right place." Only she ought to have been described by the poet whose house she had imitated:

> *"...see my breast rise*
> *Like waves of purple sea as here I stand;*
> *And how my arms are moved in wonderful wise..."*

Thus had Morris described Guinevere, yearning for the lost spring of first love but still radiant in the fulness of midsummer and using her beauty as a defense against a charge of adultery with Lancelot.

Like her countrywomen in England, she wore the hot, flaring, impractical, but magnificent skirt of the day. Under that voluminous bell, she could have hidden the hips of an elephant or a giraffe, but her bold and revealing blouse left little doubt as to the splendor of her forearms, her shoulders, and her breasts. Her gown was green satin. Below her elbows were cuffs of green brocade; and a moss-green bonnet followed the contours of her golden, backswept, downfalling hair, except where a pert white feather flared above her head. The Lady Greensleeves, he thought, and remembered with a guilty—no, guiltless—thrill that Greensleeves had been a woman of pleasure. Guinevere, Greensleeves... The two women shared more than their alliterative names, and Charlie liked both of them.

At first she made no gesture to greet him. She stared at him with unconcealed surprise and it seemed to Charlie, a concern which was strangely akin to that of Mr. Lane when the kindly old solicitor had cautioned him about accepting the position. She stepped forward slightly and extended her hand. He noticed that the movement seemed difficult for her. She moved with a kind of slow and graceful languor, and she held tightly to his hand for support. Perhaps the tropical climate had enervated her. Perhaps she had been ill with malaria or yellow fever.

A smile illuminated her face. In fact, she did not so much smile as radiate with her entire body, as if she had been suffused by the lights of a great candelabrum in a ballroom. Her skin was the pink of sweetheart roses. He looked in vain for the lines which should have marked the passage of sixteen years, including her widowhood and whatever illness had drained her of strength. But for all he could tell, she appeared to be a ripe and bountiful woman of thirty. Perhaps in this tropical climate—though because of the trade winds it was not really hot, even inside the crater—she preserved her beauty by economizing in her movements; her languor, so contrary to the bloom of her face and figure, was as deliberate as her delicately indelicate gown and her artfully artless coiffure.

"I stared at you," she smiled, "because of my good fortune and Mr. Lane's good judgment in choosing one who somehow manages to look like both an athlete and a poet at the same time. The athlete will please my daughter, and the poet will delight her mother. If it weren't for your blond hair and your considerable height, I could have taken you for John Keats."

Considerable height. How much more gracious than Mr. Lane's description of him as middling! And the comparison to Keats! Charlie was not adept at exchanging fulsome compliments, but now his words spilled forth like coins from a cornucopia.

"And I took you for Guinevere. I'm sure she had hair like yours. The color of ripe wheat. And she was beautiful and *bountiful.*"

She laughed heartily. "I take that for a compliment, though 'bountiful' has been used as a synonym for 'fat.'"

"Oh no," he protested. "I meant to say you're a stunner!"

And then, tongue-tied by his lapse into slang, he waited to be rescued by her tact.

She said quite simply, "Thank you, my dear. No one on Oleandra has ever paid me such a tribute. I've always identified a little with Guinevere. Iseult was a goddess—she lived in a book, never on earth—but Guinevere was flesh and blood. 'Tis the low sun makes the color.' You must teach my daughter about the Arthurian cycle. She disdains Malory and abhors Tennyson. I'm afraid she prefers the local folklore, with all its barbarisms."

"Where is your daughter?" A charming fancy occurred to him. If a woman between forty-five and fifty could look thirty, perhaps a girl of fifteen could look nineteen and, even if she disliked Tennyson, possess her mother's grace and naturalness instead of the affectations and airs of the girls he had known in England.

"She's with us now, I suspect. Behind a tree, in a tree, in the house staring out a window. Who can say? Probably she wanted to look you over from a distance before she meets you. Her manners could use some polishing, and I hope she overhears me. Jill! Jill! Come and meet Mr. Sorley!"

There was no answer. Silence seemed tangible in the cassia-sweet air. With a shock akin to fear, Charlie realized that in all the trees surrounding the Red House, he had seen and heard no birds. Approaching the village, yes. Even in the village, yellow-breasted sugar birds had played among the bougainvilleas and warbled their rapid and somewhat wheezing songs. But not here, not within the enchanted (bewitched?) circle of the Red House. He would have to modify his first impression of bland English charm. To Charlie a house without birds was a troubled house.

But there were still the Caribs. Even after unloading his belongings and Mrs. Meynell's supplies, they had not withdrawn into the bush where they seemed to belong. Two English servants, a stooped, sallow man, rather like a bent broomstick, and a small boy who seemed to be his son, muffled in a shapeless sack-like garment from which his bare feet protruded like the feelers of a snail, had emerged from the house, glared at the Indians, and wordlessly appropriated the belongings while the Caribs had taken up silent stations among the trees. Their sullen faces glittered with curiosity and malice. Perhaps they wished to see the confrontation between the young Englishman and the girl he had come to teach.

Mrs. Meynell followed Charlie's gaze, and Charlie watched the look which passed between her and her presumed servants and reached some intuitive conclusions. She was their mistress, yes, but they disliked her even while they served her. For her own part, she needed them to fetch her supplies from the schooner, cultivate cacao and other island crops, and tend the cottages in the village; she tolerated and controlled them—to a point. But at any moment, depending on circumstances which even Charlie's intuition could not surmise, the control might falter and fail. The Red House grew steadily less tranquil and more intriguing. He began to hope for a real adventure.

Almost curtly, she dismissed the Caribs with a flick of her wrist, or tried to dismiss them. In fact, they did not respond with the least movement; they had not yet seen what they were waiting to see. They kept to their places with a tenacity bordering on insolence.

The clapping of hands was neither loud nor prolonged; once, twice, and the Caribs were gone, and in their place stood a single native. He was not one of the rowers and porters; he was a newcomer; and to call him a Carib like his countrymen was to do him an injustice. He was tall and bronzed and fiercely beautiful, and he somehow seemed, even on this tiny island, a king. He directed his smile to Charlie, and it was as if he had said, "Welcome to my kingdom, as guest—and subject."

Then, like his men, he faded among the cassias.

"His name is Curk," Elizabeth said with a studied casualness. "He is my foreman. You will have to forgive his men for their bad manners. A stranger, especially one who has come to teach their beloved Jill, makes them curious and a little jealous. You see, she has spent a lot of time with them—far too much, in fact. I am often confined to my bed and she's thrown on her own devices. Without playmates, she goes to the Caribs. Now they feel they're losing her to an Englishman. They don't like us very much, except for Jill. Or anybody else, including each other, again with one exception—Curk, whom they adore. You might call them living anachronisms, a race that ought to be extinct but has somehow survived in spite of itself, and in a world it despises."

"You're not fair to them, Mama." It was Jill. She appeared to have dropped from a tree or come around a tree or even out of the earth. She made no apology. Unfortunately, her appearance was far less provocative than her arrival. Almost with relief Charlie realized that he was not in danger of falling in love with her. She was no competition for her mother. Though he knew her to be about fifteen, she looked at the moment even younger, a tomboy this side of puberty, dressed in cut-off sailor trousers and middy blouse, her hair like a nest constructed by an untidy bird.

"You're not fair at all," she continued. "You hold it against them that they won't live in your cottages and take baths and plant gardens. I keep telling you, they're happy in the mangrove swamp, and dirt to them isn't something to be washed off."

There were redeeming features to the girl. Her skin was a rich, deep brown—it was not an English complexion but it was not unbecoming—and her green eyes possessed almost an Oriental slant which would have seemed mysterious and alluring had she dressed to accentuate them and combed her tawny hair. She was, in brief, probably a pretty girl who had managed to disguise her prettiness and, almost, her sex.

There seemed nothing calculated about her guise. There was no hint of posing, or of a wish to shock. It was as if she did not know that girls were expected to look like girls. She dressed as she chose, and she chose to dress like a scrawny pirate lad. Even her movements were quick, brusque, and boyish. In total contrast to her mother, there were no softnesses about her body, no undulations about her movements. She needed a tutor for more than biology and poetry. Why had she not observed and imitated so radiant and utterly feminine a mother?

When Mrs. Meynell failed to pursue the argument about the Caribs, Jill turned to Charlie. "I dislike French. I'll study it only because of the boats that come in from Martinique—I like to talk to the sailors—but you'll have to prod me with the grammar. I'm very good at biology, though. I can teach you some things about life in the sea. And how to dress on Oleandra. I keep telling Mother not to wear those absurd skirts. But she will look like the ladies in England. And you—What are those ridiculous tweeds and boots you're wearing? And the bowler hat with the feather about to take flight?"

"They're my bicycling outfit," said Charlie, crestfallen. He had really not known how a young man should dress on Oleandra and he had chosen his jauntiest outfit. But Jill had a point; a tweed coat, braided trousers, and Hessian boots, however jaunty in England, were merely hot in the tropics. "What should I wear?"

"What I do," she said. "You can pick up some sailor togs from the schooner next month."

"We don't want two sailors in the house," Mrs. Meynell said tartly. "Some of my husband's old linens can be altered to fit Mr. Sorley, though he looks very nice as he is."

"If you like ruddy English schoolboys who learn how to win battles on the playing fields of Eton."

Charlie forced a smile. "In my case, Marlborough, and my first battle is not yet won." He was trying to like her in spite of her absolute refusal to be gracious, but he found himself withholding judgment; he must learn what frustrations explained her incivilities. "I'm sure you can teach me a great deal about the Caribbean. Just an hour ago I mistook a dolphin for a shark."

Her eyes brightened. "You're sure it wasn't a shark? There are all kinds in the waters around the island. Real beauties. Hammerheads, especially, but also blue sharks and tigers. Usually the dolphins keep their distance."

"No, it was a dolphin all right. We became friends while the Caribs rowed me ashore."

"He won't last long in *these* waters," she predicted happily. "Not with all those sharks."

"Oh, he was a lovable dolphin. You wouldn't want anything to happen to him." Not only was he finding it hard, as yet, to like her, he was finding it hard not to dislike her.

She grimaced. "They're such ugly creatures. And so vicious. Have you ever seen a shark battered to death by dolphins? They ram him from all sides until he's a bloody pulp."

"My sympathies would be with the dolphins. After all, the sharks kill their calves."

"That's because you're sentimental. A dolphin knows how to play up to a man. To get his attention with tricks. Leaping and gamboling and catching fish in mid-air and all that. You probably believe those silly stories about dolphins rescuing sailors. But at heart they're the most vicious creatures in the sea."

"I don't think so at all," he snapped, wishing for the big hickory cane which had belonged to the headmaster at Marlborough. If she dressed like a boy and talked like a bully, a good caning was exactly what she deserved. "The one I saw today—"

"Come into the house now. Mother's not used to being on her feet so long."

He looked at Mrs. Meynell. The color had left her face, but not, it seemed to him, from weariness. She was looking at her daughter with a kind of disgust and despair.

"Jill has a curious sense of—affection," she said in a dead voice. "I hope you change her tastes."

"Or I'll change his," Jill laughed. "What'll I call you? Charles or Charlie?"

It was the one time in his life when he stood on his dignity. No one who disliked dolphins could use his given name.

"You may call me 'Mr. Sorley.'"

They walked into the house.

And no birds sang.

CHAPTER FOUR

I emerged from a tortuous and torturous passage into a brilliance of sunlight and green water. I was used to blue lagoons which reflected the sky and black lagoons so deep that they seemed to have swallowed the sky. But green. It had borrowed the hue of young palm fronds and it spoke of the land and not the sea; it spoke to me.

On one end, a mangrove swamp enticed me with many canals; on the other was a beach of powder-fine black sand, expressly created for swimmers like Charlie to rest and sunbathe after they had frolicked in the water with a dolphin. I had heard of such beaches, black instead of pink or white, but soft to the toe or the eye, from dolphins who had visited Tahiti.

The other sides of the lagoon were less inviting. I leaped repeatedly until I had chiseled a clear sculpture of them in my brain. Sheer walls, like titan faces bewhiskered with foliage, reared toward the sky. One such face was broken by a ledge, perhaps a hundred feet above the water. I shuddered as if I had suddenly spilled from the Gulf Stream into the cold Atlantic, for I knew its name: The Ledge Which Looms Like a Shark. Its stone configurations, even its gaping jaws, not only deserved the name but (according to my informant, the Old Bull) served the Caribs in their rituals honoring shark-headed Tark, their national deity.

There was no trace of a shark in the lagoon, however. My superlatively developed sonar sense would have warned me of any such presence immediately. I peered, I exercised my nostrils, I opened my mouth and allowed the water to flow across my sensitive taste buds. All in all, and in spite of the ominous-looking ledge, I loved what I had found. I could not return to the land and reverse the disastrous course of my ancestors, but I could at least surround myself with land and reduce the encompassment of the sea. What was more, in my leaps I had seen the little English cottages climbing the crater wall, and above them, flaunting its chimneys and flashing its red bricks in the afternoon sun, the house of Mrs. Meynell and my new friend, Charlie; the Red House inspired by William Morris.

You understand that at this time I did not know about contemporary human poets and designers like Morris. We dolphins only know what we hear and see and what our elders have known and seen. I knew about Shakespeare and his play The Tempest. I knew about Milton's Paradise Lost, which seemed to me a parable of the dolphins and their exile from the land. Later I overheard Charlie giving Jill some of her lessons, and of course he often talked to me, even though it was a long time until he learned that I could understand him. Since dolphins are born historians, we pick up facts as naturally and quickly as we capture slow-swimming prawns in our open jaws. It is due to our not being able to write, and having to remember things. Now, thanks to Charlie, I can list the works of Lord Tennyson and dear Mrs. Browning (Charlie's favorite), as well as Morris. What is more, I can tell you every king and queen of England, wicked or good, beloved or beheaded, and what poets flourished in whose reigns.

I swam and leapt until I was exhausted, memorizing the contours of this, my new home, remembering distances, gauging relationships between the lagoon and the land. I found the water remarkably fresh, considering its single outlet to the sea, and abundant with pompano, lobsters, crabs, angel fish, and small octopi, with an occasional man-of-war which I scrupulously avoided. Yesterday, I would have fed as I wandered, and wandered with listless flippers and unobservant eyes. Today I was too excited to feed. Once I had ascertained the abundance of food, I proceeded to the mangrove swamp and discovered a maze of canals, and tiny islets where dirt had collected around the roots of the thick-grown plants and occasional land bridges evidently made by men. There was one path which led straight from the edge of the lagoon, where three dugout canoes had been upended and covered with palm fronds, through the swamp, and up the slope toward the Red House. Bordering this path (or should I say littering?) were the palm-thatched huts of the Caribs, whom Mrs. Meynell had been unable to entice into her cleanly cottages. Naked babies waded in the canals or played among a refuse of coconut shells and banana peels, and slatternly women snoozed on straw pallets which they had arranged in the shade as far as possible from their children. Had I been a shark, I could have taken my pick of the wading babies, though in spite of their plumpness they were much too dirty—squalid is the word—to be appetizing.

Throughout my explorations, I lost no chance of leaping from the water to observe the Red House, with the hope that Charlie would appear in the great arch of the door and spy me in the lagoon. But it was not until the second day that he finally emerged from the house. He had changed his manner of dress. In place of the bicycling outfit he had worn on his arrival, he now wore sky-blue bell-bottom trousers, with an open shirt and a red scarf. He looked down at the lagoon and as I spun madly in midair I saw that I had caught his eye. He moved to descend the cliff. But almost at once a slender figure—boy or girl, I could not say—stepped from the house, beckoned commandingly, almost insolently, it seemed to me, and Charlie stopped in his tracks. The figure was indeterminate, the shape was slim and girlish though without any perceptible bosom, but the clothes were male: the pants of a sailor cut off below the knees, a kind of middy blouse, and neither shoes nor sandals. Sailor, did I say? I might have said pirate. Immediately I disliked it. Anything gotten up so strangely meant no good to Charlie or me; besides, it was keeping him from his visit to me. But my distaste ran deeper than jealousy. It was touched with fear. My third eye saw more than it liked.

The figure took Charlie by the arm and attempted to lead him into the house. He pointed vehemently to the lagoon, to me, spinning through my endless somersaults. I was too distant to follow their conversation. The figure shrugged as if to say, "You're not going to climb the crater to see a dolphin, are you?" He nodded.

"Yes," he seemed to say, "that's exactly what I'm going to do." The figure spun away from him and stalked into the house. Of course it was Jill, the girl I have already described to you in an earlier episode. He followed her into the house. Really, he had no choice. Her mother had engaged him. Still, I felt betrayed. I did not like young girls to look like scrawny boys, and being a dolphin with beautiful undulating curves, I felt that a girl of Jill's apparent age—to judge by her height—should have at least the rudiments of a bosom. It was not her appearance, though, which troubled me most. It was something which I can only call her aura. Not that she was necessarily evil, but she had at least been touched by evil.

When Charlie disappeared into the house, I felt as if he had been swallowed, like a seal by a killer whale. All those pretty red bricks—old bricks brought at great expense from England; those three handsome gables, the stately chimneys and the door like an archway into a cathedral; they seemed to shut him into a prison, all the more threatening because of its pretty façade, and I had to stay in that other prison, the water, and brood about our mutual helplessness.

All day I circled the lagoon, exhausting myself by leaping to view the house, skirting the shore in case Charlie eluded his charge and came exploring. Finally, the next afternoon, I was rewarded for my vigilance. Perhaps he had left her occupied with lessons—memorizing kings or lines of poetry. At any rate, he left the house with the confident stride of one who knows his destination. Joyfully he clambered down the side of the crater, taking an occasional tumble over a banyan root, rising to resume his descent without even bothering to brush off his clothes.

Breathlessly I watched his progress (I can hold my breath for a good twenty minutes), expecting all the way that Jill would change her mind about the lesson and follow him or send a Carib after him. But no, he made his way to the bottom of the cliff and followed the dry, raised path among the mangrove trees. I lost sight of him for a time and hoped that those dirty little Carib children would not gawk at him or pelt him with indian cigars, the fruit of the mangrove. It was not long before, apparently unpelted, he reached the end of the path and the edge of the water and gave a huge, buoyant cry. Suddenly I felt a surprising shyness and made myself as unobtrusive as possible under the water. Have you ever anticipated a meeting with great enthusiasm and then, once it approaches, feared that it will be a disappointment, that you may appear ridiculous rather than enthusiastic?

He blithely stripped off his clothes and dove into the lagoon. I must confess to a certain surprise. I was not accustomed to seeing young English gentlemen remove their clothes. Caribs, yes. Sailors from any country yes. But not English boys like Charlie. I could fancy the Carib slatterns crouching behind the mangroves to ogle and ridicule his (to their eyes) pallid skin. But no bushes crackled and the slatterns were doubtless asleep along with their urchins. Another reservation occurred to me. If Charlie wished to strip, that was his privilege, but how did I know that, thus vulnerable, he was safe in these unfamiliar waters? He was a northerner who knew nothing of the tropics. I had seen no sharks, but one might yet discover the entrance from the sea; and a man-of-war, of which I had seen a number, could sting him into unconsciousness. Well, I would just have to scout for him, guide him, protect him. First, though, we must get re-acquainted. I was sadly aware that all dolphins of the same size, unless they happen to be albinos, look the same to most humans. What is more they are usually miscalled porpoises (who are distant cousins without our "bottle-noses"). In the first place, he probably would not recognize me from yesterday in this totally different location.

In the second place, even if he did, it was one thing to pat a dolphin's head when you are on the land, another to meet him nose to bottle-nose in his own element.

Stroking with grace and power, like one who had traversed many a Thames or Severn, he sped away from the shore. With alarm I saw that he meant to swim the entire half mile to the beach. Those English schoolboys! There is nothing they will not do to test their skill. Not that half a mile is any great distance, but it might prove dangerous in a lagoon which was totally unknown to him. Tangling with a man-of-war can be worse than painful; it can be fatal for a swimmer far from shore. I eased around him in a large circle so that I would not crowd and frighten him. He recognized me at once and began to tread water. What is more, he smiled. Such prompt recognition was flattering to say the least. Since I possessed no distinguishing physical characteristics, except for my slight inclination to plumpness, it must have been sheer mental rapport. Waving happily, he swam toward me and I advanced to meet him.

Soon we were face to face. The golden aureole of his hair was subdued by the water and clung about his ears like seaweed, but his splendor was undiminished. Had he possessed a tail, I might have mistaken him for the Great Triton. He did not so much swim as glitter through the water; he should have been attended by mermaids and mermen and whales like moving islands; conch shells should blow to announce his coming and the waters should part to ease his path. It is curious—and also sad—that to dolphins, men look distinguished if not, as in Charlie's case, downright Olympian, while to men a dolphin looks merely humorous. Our large snouts, however versatile, are hard to take seriously, and our fishlike contours remind men of something they catch on hooks and fry for the table.

There was an inevitable awkwardness when we met: young man and dolphin; land and sea. If he had been a dolphin like me, I would have tumbled about with him in a merry scramble, nudging, tickling, flipping. If I had been a young man like him, he would have shaken my hand or clapped me on the shoulder. As it was, we were both at a loss as to how to communicate a greeting. It was Charlie who found a way. He simply reached out and, treading water, placed his hand on my head in a gesture of uncondescending salutation.

In response, I squeaked, "Rest now. Then we'll swim and get acquainted," though I knew that my words would seem to Charlie nothing more than noises emitted through my airhole. At least I hoped that they would put him at ease; that he could grasp my good intentions from my intonations.

Needless to say, however, I could understand practically everything Charlie said to me, since dolphins have been overhearing and understanding swimmers and divers and sailors and beachcombers for several thousand years. I myself can understand eleven human languages and also readily converse with sperm whales and sea turtles.

When he spoke, it was for the same reason that I had spoken to him.

"You can't understand me," he said, "but I know that dolphins have ears, much prettier than mine, since they don't stick out"—leave it to tactful Charlie to notice my ears instead of my snout—"and I just feel like talking to you because, well, because I want to talk to someone who's sympathetic."

Sympathetic. That was his exact word to me. To selfish Gloomer, who had thought about nothing and nobody but himself since his mother had died. Well, Charlie changed all that just by thinking the best of me.

"It's funny. I can't speak with the people in the house. Mrs. Meynell rests most of the time and Jill talks most of the time about sharks and battles. I can talk to you, though, and it doesn't matter if you don't know what I'm saying. If you did, you'd understand, and that's what matters."

There were big tears in his eyes. This stocky, manly boy was about to cry. He ducked to erase the tears and emerged with a smile.

"What a windbag I am! Let's have a swim." He let go of me and resumed his passage across the lagoon. Since I had appointed myself his protector, it seemed the propitious moment to teach him how to ride me. Metaphorically speaking, it was the best way to keep him under my flipper. In the old Greek sculptures, the boy is shown clutching the dolphin's back, legs wrapped around the body. Such a conception represents the error of sculptors who had never ridden dolphins nor seen them ridden. Certainly it was not the way Anon rode the dolphin or dolphins who rescued him from the pirates. It is not by tail and flippers alone that we manage to swim with the speed of a shark and the zest of a seal. We have to be free to wriggle our entire bodies.

My problem was two-fold first I had to convey to Charlie that he ought to ride me; second, how to ride me. I caught his foot in my beak and interrupted his swim. He turned and surveyed me over his shoulder with some astonishment. Another joke? The shark masquerade repeated? An invitation to horseplay? (Forgive my zoologically misleading word.) He was not angry, but he was just this side of impatience. I released the foot and immediately darted under him and rose under his legs. Now he understood that I was offering him a ride. My first problem was solved. But he clutched me so tightly that he almost sank both of us. I could neither breathe nor advance. I shook clear of him, dipped, and rose under him so gently that I did not so much lift as ease him out of the water. This time he held me much less tightly but still his legs hampered my movements.

Dolphins pride themselves on their smooth, sensitive skin—never a barnacle on us—and Charlie's arms and legs, though muscular, were neither abrasive nor bruising. In fact, it was as if he were giving me a big, friendly embrace; he seemed a part of the land warming me momentarily from the wetness and sliminess of the sea I disliked. But remember, I am still a youth, and I lacked the skill to swim with my body enwrapped, however lightly, by two strapping legs. Once more I dislodged him, faced him directly, and wriggled my dorsal fin in a manner to suggest the part of me which I meant for him to grasp. He delivered an "ah" of comprehension, grasped the fin with amazingly sensitive fingers for such a sturdy hand, and off I sped, his body gliding above me. To an observer on the shore it must have looked as if he were lying directly on my back; in truth, I was drawing him through the water.

The beach loomed up at us like the side view of a long black whale and Charlie, quite breathless from excitement, and I, equally breathless because of my burden, parted company in shallow water. He patted my head and clambered on to the fine, squishing sand. By this time his nakedness seemed to me entirely natural. After all, I never wear clothes, and why should men—even English gentlemen—wear them in a warm lagoon? He shook the water from his golden hair and threw back his head to catch the sun in his face and, though his body was a little pale from England and thus a sharp contrast to the black sand, it was already pinkening from the tropical sun (I had to find a way to warn him about sunburn). If Apollo instead of Aphrodite had been born in the sea, he would have climbed ashore with just such supple and unselfconscious grace.

Then I heard a laugh. The indeterminate person from the Red House (I saw now that she was a young girl of fifteen or so; it is hard to be exact about the age of young human females, since they all look much the same to me except for their bosoms—or lack thereof) was standing on the beach and shaking with laughter. She was disfigured as usual (I refuse to say dressed) by fisherman's trousers cut off at the knees, and an old shirt which a Carib would have been ashamed to wear and which failed to conceal the fact that if she had any breasts, they resembled lemons instead of coconuts. A lady would not have appeared in such garb. Furthermore, a lady would have absented herself when faced by a naked gentleman. Was she trying to pass for a pirate lad?

Charlie turned and, without the least discomposure, retraced his steps into the water. When he was covered to his waist, he turned to face her. He seemed to forget that the water was transparent.

"I thought you were Odysseus washed ashore by the storm," she taunted.

"If you're Nausicaä, I suggest you disappear with your maidens to study your French. You were supposed to read two lessons in the grammar."

"You've already given me an anatomy lesson. I've always wondered if Englishmen were like Caribs. Besides, you're not old enough to be Odysseus, and I'm not decorous enough to be a princess. If you insist on the French, you'll have to give me some help with the irregular verbs. From what I've heard of French novels, I think you're dressed exactly right."

He forced himself to sound very stern and tutorial. "Young ladies do not read French novels. Not the kind in yellow covers, I mean. The kind you seem to mean."

Then, with infinite dignity (though I could see that he was smothering a chuckle) he turned his back on her, grasped my dorsal fin, and we began to re-cross the lagoon.

"Wait, Mr. Sorley," she called after him. "I'll fetch you some clothes."

He pretended not to hear her.

"Mr. Sorley, I command you to wait."

Charlie always did prefer older women.

CHAPTER FIVE

His room was austerely but tastefully furnished. What had William Morris said? Let objects be few, functional and beautiful. There was a dressing table of plain oak and a marble-topped washstand. A massive settle, a pillowless bench with sides and back as tall as a standing man and embellished with medieval maidens playing dulcimers, dominated the room, pleased the eye, and functioned no doubt for those with generously padded backbones, but Charlie was a little sore from his swim in the lagoon and deplored the lack of cushions. He climbed into his nightdress and then into his bed, a large canopied affair, its curtains intertwined with lilies and blades of grass. Should he draw the curtains? No. Though the night was cool, such a gesture seemed a confession of cowardice— a shutting out of whatever vaguely but tangibly frightened him about the island on this his second night; a shutting in of his loneliness and grief. And yet he permitted himself to snuggle into his pillows like a field mouse burrowing from a hawk; that luxury, that escape seemed allowable under the circumstances and he tried not to wish directly for sleep, because the wish would soon grow insistent and keep him awake all night. He must surprise that most precious and precariously held of possessions, that brief respite from the day's glare and the night's woundings. Think about Jill and wonder if she were twelve or fifteen or ageless. About Mrs. Meynell and wonder if the bright daylight would reveal blemishes in her seemingly flawless skin. About the dolphin he had met in the sea and then again in the lagoon and their strange, almost instantaneous sense of kinship. (You see, from the very first he returned my affection; I have his own assurances.)

Barefooted, shuffling, his little form inundated by his large hooded robe, Telesphorus entered the room with a pair of candles; one to light his way, one to leave with Charlie.

"Mistress say you will need two candle to read by." He was an English boy, but reared in the islands with indian playmates, and his voice was soft, his grammar relaxed, and he tended to slur and run together his words like the Negroes Charlie had seen on Martinique. It was a speech which suited a leisurely life in the tropics, where to sleep through the afternoon was considered a necessity instead of an indolence, and no one ran when he could walk unless he was being pursued by a fer-de-lance.

Charlie thought guiltily that he ought to be reading the third chapter in that abominable grammar he was trying to teach Jill.

"Thank you, Telesphorus. Tell your mistress I'm grateful for her thoughtfulness."

Telesphorus looked carefully around the room, at Charlie, at the bed, at the books scattered on the settle, and seemed to feel that he could depart and carry a good report to the mistress about the studiousness of the new tutor.

"Will tell Mistress. Master too."

"The Master, you say?" Mr. Meynell had been dead some fifteen years. "Do you mean your father?"

"No."

"Are there other servants who give you orders?" He had been puzzled at the seeming lack of them in so large and fine a house.

"Five of them once. All go back to England. Now Caribs come to clean when Master allow."

"But who is the Master you keep mentioning?" His exasperation was hard to contain.

"Lives in village. Back of cannons." And then he was gone, like a candle snuffed by a sudden wind.

"Mr. Sorley."

He woke with a jolt. Yes, he had actually fallen asleep after Telesphorus' departure. He might, for a change, have slept all night had he not been awakened by Jill. He could not be vexed with her, however, when he saw the fragile face lit by a single taper, the tanned skin beneath hair as fine and silvery as a spider's web. Jill in the evening, it seemed, was not the strident tomboy of the afternoon.

"Mr. Sorley, my mother wishes to see you."

"Now?" The hour was late, if he could judge by his half-burned candle.

"At once. She is ill, you see. She has taken a spell."

"But Telesphorus and his father—" It was not drowsiness which kept him from wanting to visit Mrs. Meynell in her bed, nor even propriety; it was something which he dared not try to define.

She made a gesture of contempt. "They have no understanding."

"I'll follow you," he said. "First, I must"—and here he stammered—"I must put on my trousers."

She laughed and tugged on his arm. "I'm an island girl. I don't know your English niceties. Come as you are. All I can see are your feet, and I saw much more this afternoon. Here are some slippers I've brought. So now you're as muffled as a corpse laid out for burial." Again, the disquieting Jill, brazen of gesture, macabre of speech.

He followed her down the hall; she was careful to keep ahead of him, not out of deference to his modesty, he supposed, but in her haste to reach her mother. His slippers slapped the bare wooden floor with little hollow taps.

He wondered why he had been embarrassed by his nightdress in front of this strange, wild girl, who had not in the least embarrassed him that afternoon on the beach. In England, it was true, in a country house, if there was only one bathroom to a suite of bedrooms and guests met in the halls by accident at night, they politely averted their eyes and did not speak. But he was not in England and his hostess of the moment, in spite of her English parenthood, had proclaimed herself a child of the islands. Perhaps it was the vulnerability which had briefly marked her when she first awoke him. Then it was as if she, and not he, had been the one surprised in an unguarded and revealing gentleness.

Mrs. Meynell's canopied bed, with its damask curtains flowered with the golden sunflowers so beloved by the Pre-Raphaelites, reminded him of the great red tent of a queen—Guinevere? Iseult?—who had come to watch her lover joust in a tournament. His fancies were not in the least diminished by the practical observation that the feet of the bed were set in little pails of water to prevent the encroachment of ants or spiders.

The scent of laudanum was strong in the air, at once acrid and sickeningly sweet. The powerful, sleep-inducing drug was freely dispensed in most apothecary shops. But such quantities as he smelled in the room indicated addiction. He thought of Elizabeth Barrett languishing in her sickbed with drugs and dreams; waiting for the robust poet who would free her from the twin tyrannies of a harsh father and a mysterious malady.

Jill paused in the door, her face a curious complexity for one so young. Compassion for her mother's apparent pain. Surprise and envy at the summoning of a stranger in the middle of the night when she, the daughter, stood ready to comfort her mother.

Through the open curtains of her bed, Mrs. Meynell spoke drowsily but with quiet authority.

"Thank you, Jill. You may go now. Your robe is thin. The trade winds are chilly at night."

"Shall I come back to fetch Mr. Sorley?"

"He can find his own way back."

Mrs. Meynell motioned him beside her on the bed. She smiled at his hesitation.

"In the islands we forget the amenities. I am an invalid, you see. Do you think I feel compromised if a young gentleman, young enough to be my son, sits beside me on my sick bed? Should he feel compromised? Think of me as Elizabeth Barrett before her marriage to Robert. You've come to administer a medicine or prescribe a trip to Italy for my health, or simply to keep me company through another sleepless night."

His hesitation was momentary. He was not a prude but a poet, and Mrs. Meynell's mention of the Brownings seemed to him to border on the clairvoyant and to augur the development of a devoted friendship. Furthermore, she was disarmingly young and beautiful in the light of the candelabrum, a rosette of mischievous angels, which swung from the ceiling. By daylight she had looked a ripe thirty; by candlelight, an intoxicating twenty-five.

She took his hand and held it against her forehead. She was damp and cold.

"You're having a chill," he cried.

"Loneliness is chilling, my dear. But you must know that already, better than I." Her beauty was flawless even at closest range.

"Yes. Yes, I know."

"Loneliness is like a sea anemone writhing in your entrails. Nobody knows it's there but you. But it grows and wounds and finally devours you."

The slight coarseness of her speech, the word "entrails," unthinkable in England except among women of the lower classes, did not trouble him in the least; rather, he was fascinated by her total disregard for the dictates of the society into which they had both been born and which, apparently, they had both withstood.

"You lost your husband some years ago, didn't you?"

"Lost him? Yes, but it was what I found which—" She broke off suddenly and squeezed his hand with desperate tenderness. Her amber eyes reminded him of honeycombs. Why did he also think, momentarily and guiltily, of bees and stingers, of pride and the power to wound?

"May I bring you some medicine?" he asked with real concern.

"I have a cabinet of medicines. I have two servants and a daughter to administer them. I have already taken my nightly dose of laudanum. But your arrival—first on the island, then in my room—has excited me beyond sleep. Sit here and talk to me. Medicine me with words. Your voice is very soothing, you know. Deep and manly, but gentle and young, so young. It's like the rain falling on oleander leaves. Are you truly gentle, Mr. Sorley?"

"Sometimes impatient, I'm afraid."

"When? With whom? With me for fetching you out of a warm bed in the middle of the night?"

"Never with you," he said, almost with vehemence. "How could I be angry with you? With myself, I meant. Most of all, with circumstances."

"But circumstances—those beyond our control—are indeed maddening. Impatience is a very tiny and quite forgivable sin in such cases. Now we shall forget our sins and talk of happy things. Our tropical nights seem longer than those in England, don't they? Sometimes I feel quite maddened by tree-frogs or the wind in the casuarina trees. Talk to me, Mr. Sorley, and we shall pass the night together."

"You surely don't want to hear the adventures of a schoolboy. You know, till now I've never been out of school. First Marlborough, then a year at Cambridge."

She pressed his hand with maternal ardor. "Poor little school boy thrust out into the sinful world." Was there a touch of irony in her words? "I should never have sent for you. I had no way of knowing how innocent you were. I had expected a hard, brawling fellow, educated—yes, after all, he had to teach my daughter—but dogged by gambling debts and enemies, and likely as not, dispossessed by his father for excessive wenching."

"Whatever you expected, I'm glad I came. I found more than I had expected."

"Yes, I'm afraid you did," she sighed. "Much, much more. Now talk to me about England. The Lake Country. The downs around Marlborough. The incredible greenness of the trees along the Thames. I know about your mother and your brother and I grieve for you. But now I want countrysides, oaks and not palms, heather and not sea-grapes. Winters and hearthfires and snow on the roof. Changing seasons—how precious they are. There are no seasons here. Except that one still grows old, and it's more of a shock because the leaves don't redden and fall, there isn't any cycle in nature to reflect the change. There are only mirrors. But here I am growing morbid again. And what did you love the most in England?"

"Walking the downs near Marlborough in the autumn. Digging among the leaves for mounds where the fairies live—the Irish call them Sidhe."

"Do you believe in the Sidhe?"

"Yes." His ancestors were Celts and his answer was unequivocal. He was not being figurative or fanciful. He was telling her the literal truth. She was not a woman to whom one lied, though she might be a woman, he reflected, who told one lies.

"They're still there—in their mounds?"

"I don't think so. I think they've gone away. Gone somewhere else where people still believe in them."

"No, my dear," she said with finality. "Every land has its Sidhe, its Dark Ones. They're much too strong, proud, clever to flee. You see, they know how to hide when people cease to honor them. When the church speaks out against them. The Little People, they're called. But of course they aren't little at all. They're just hard to recognize through their disguises. Thus they can work their evil so secretly that people think them small, if people think about them at all. But when they choose to be seen, they are...monstrous. Whatever their names, every land has them."

"You've seen them?"

The change in her was instantaneous. Like Jill, she sometimes seemed to be several persons. She laughed a quick bitter laugh. "It's the late hour. The fancies of childhood are coming back to me. No, I haven't seen them. Your mounds near Marlborough are not their dwellings at all, but tombs for the old warriors. The Sidhe never existed except in our nightmares. And here on Oleandra we can leave them to the superstitious Caribs..."

He wanted to argue for the existence of Sidhe, fairies, gnomes, Tritons, Centaurs. He wanted to argue that they were not so much evil as unmoral; that they loved and warred without violating any moral code because they were not concerned with morality. But arguments would only disturb her. She had dismissed such beings from the conversation and, as it were, from the earth.

"And when you walk on the downs, what do you think about? London? Girls? Latin declensions for the next examination?" Though the bed was large, she was cosily close to him. He was sure that on first alighting he had allowed a decorous distance between them.

"I make up poetry," he said without embarrassment. At Marlborough they had called him The Poet out of admiration, not derision, because like William Morris and John Keats he had been as quick with his fists as with a couplet or a quatrain. He had once throttled a fellow for snickering at one of his sonnets.

"Love poetry? Nature poetry?"

"No," he corrected her. "I've never been in love so I don't try to write about it yet. And everybody writes about nature. Wordsworth quite turned me against daffodils. I write about the Celts and the Romans and the Saxons and the Normans. Bardic poetry. Battle poetry. Epic poetry, you might say, only I haven't finished a whole epic yet. I've only done two thousand lines of one."

"Your choice of subjects is highly commendable—Jill will be fascinated—but I don't feel like trumpets and clarions tonight. Tomorrow you shall recite your fragmentary epic to me. Tonight…tonight I should like something sweet, plaintive, melancholy. The nightingale and not the war hawk."

"I'm not a nightingale myself but what if I quoted some lines by Tennyson I learned at Marlborough? I thought them silly at the time, but they seem to have grown on me."

"I suspect you've grown on them. Go ahead." He quoted with the fervor of his own grief:

"Tears, idle tears, I know not what they mean;
Tears from the depth of some divine despair
Rise in the heart, and gather to the eyes,
In looking on the happy autumn-fields
And thinking of the days that are no more."

"Our beloved Laureate. Now he's our greatest poet, but the days that are no more are much more precious to him than the Laureateship or audiences with the Queen. The days at Cambridge. The days with his friend Hallam. His tears weren't idle at all, were they?"

She took him in her arms as naturally as a mother enfolds her child. She was beautiful like his own mother, with the sweet rounded softness of a Madonna, and then with delectable guilt he realized that she was not so much a Madonna as a Titian Venus, soft and rounded, yes, but for cradling Mars and not the Christ child. She appeared to him less maternal by the second.

Though inexperienced, he had read the poems of Algernon Swinburne and a large number of French novels and with gentle reluctance he disengaged himself from her embrace.

She laughed. "My little virgin. You've never known a woman, have you?"

Why had she twice called him little? Why did she not see that he was medium in height, even if not tall, and stocky of build, rather like the William Morris she so much admired? A good wrestler, a good climber. No softness anywhere.

And why had she called him "virgin" with seeming disdain? Victorian boys of nineteen were expected to be virgins, but some of his friends had been taken to Places by their fathers, given a knowing nudge in the ribs, and left in the custody of a plump, painted woman. She had grinned hugely and, acting half maternal, half businesslike, presented them to a line of simpering women in their thirties who looked like girls until you got close to them. Still, they were real "stunners" in bed, his friends had boasted, and later they had gone back on their own, and the secret was one between them and their fathers and carefully guarded from their mothers and of course from the girls they later married. Mrs. Meynell obviously knew about such places and approved of them.

"Dear Mr. Sorley," she smiled. "You didn't know you had been engaged—lured all the way from England—by a fallen woman, did you? You didn't realize the full extent of your duties."

"My duties," he said manfully, "are to tutor Jill in French, biology, poetry, and related subjects."

"And nothing left for her mother? No wisdom to impart? No biology? No related subjects? Nothing to learn from her mother? No wisdom to be imparted?"

"You've already taught me something," he said. "If you're a fallen woman, I think I like them better than the other kind. Certainly they're prettier and better educated, and they make excellent conversation. With girls my age, I just sit around and talk about summering at Bath or the next Season in London, and all I can do with them is waltz or walk in a garden. I kissed a girl once behind a grape arbor, and she was obviously enjoying herself, until her sister found us and then she slapped me and ordered me never to call on her again. Another time, I told a girl she had a pretty ankle and she stomped on my foot. It seems I wasn't supposed to have seen her ankle. Or maybe I was supposed to see it but not say anything. I don't know what you think you fell from, but I would call you a climbed woman. I always did like Lucifer better than Michael."

"If you're Lucifer, why don't you tempt me? I shall be your Eve."

"Lilith," he said. "Eve was a bit of a simpleton. She had no mind of her own. Whoever was with her at the moment—God, Adam, snake—was her master."

She looked at him with pleasure and also with a question. His speech had clearly pleased and flattered her. But where did she stand with him? Was he merely bantering with her or was he ready to yield to her blandishments?

He looked not at her but into his heart, pleased because he had managed to save her pride, drawn to her by her learning, loveliness, and sadness, wondering if at last he had begun, just begun, to fall in love with her. It was the wondering—the necessity to wonder at such a time—which restrained him. She desired him; he desired her; but perhaps he would overwhelmingly come to love her, and he must save the gift of his body for the moment of certainty. For it was, after all, though to him unremarkable, a gift. Wenches had beckoned to him in the street. A flower girl had whispered a secret address and a girl in the strand had cracked nuts between her teeth and laughed an invitation: "Now there's a proper gentleman from 'is 'ead to 'is toes. But I could teach 'im a thing or three." He had resisted these multiple temptations, not out of fear and not with the abstinence of a priest or a saint, but because he wanted his first love to be his only love, and the one gift he had to offer besides his heart was his body, firm, clean, and chaste. Unlike practically everyone who met him, he did not think of himself as a handsome boy, but at least he would be, well, like a clean-growing fir tree without any broken branches and without any rot. His mother had been a goddess to him; his brother had been his closest friend, perfectly understood, perfectly understanding. Having known the highest in family love, he did not intend to accept less than the highest in the love of a man for a woman.

He took her hand and kissed it with a warm, firm pressure, courteously yet not without passion. That was his answer. It was not yet time. He saw that she understood; that she was disappointed but not wounded; he was postponing her, not rejecting her.

"Very well," she said with a little gesture of futility. She had a way of making a kind of butterfly-shape in the air with her hands. "Go if you must. But I shan't sleep if you leave me."

"Neither shall I," he confessed.

She called after him as he reached the door:

> *"Remember me when I am gone away,*
> *Gone far away into the silent land..."*

He turned in the door and continued the poem.

> *"When you can no more hold me by the hand,*
> *Nor I half turn to go yet turning stay..."*

"Christina Rossetti," she said softly. "She loved two men. But chastely. That kind of love is possible too, my dear. Stay with me a little, Charlie." The change to his given name was natural and touching. To his playmates and schoolmasters he had been Sorley; to his mother and brother, Charlie. "As my friend and nothing more. Will you do that for me, my dear?"

When he hesitated, she smiled mischievously. "Could one of your girlfriends have quoted Christina Rossetti to you? The one you kissed behind the grape arbor?"

"All she could quote was the first stanza of 'I Wandered Lonely As a Cloud.' I've always disliked it. What's lonely about a cloud? If you had quoted Wordsworth, I would have kept on going."

He came into her arms as gratefully as a bear to its winter cave. She was redolent not of laudanum but of frangipani, exquisite and penetrating. He did not change his original resolve; he was content or at least resigned merely to lie with her in his arms, loving but not her lover, in a sweet and unassuageable yearning. She was Helen and Annabelle Lee and

Ligeia and all those other sad, shadowy women of Edgar Allan Poe. She was his Lady of Frangipanis.

He seemed to walk into sleep, and the path was soft with leaves and petals. A little boy and his mother were exploring a great garden.

"Look, Mother. The air is held up with birds!"

"It's the air that holds the birds up," she had laughed.

"Never mind. There's every color of a peacock's tail. Like the one in the London Zoo. Blue and red and—what's that color, Mother?"

"Indigo."

"I-n-d-i-g-o." He spoke each letter distinctly, relishing it, then putting them together into a new word which he would never forget. "Indigo. I like it best of all. It seems to have fallen out of a sunset."

When he awoke, the windows were brimming with light like three tall sun-gods come to awaken him.

But Elizabeth, unlike the lady in Shakespeare's sonnet, outshone the sun. Even in the dishevelment of her awakening, she stirred him with her beauty.

"My lovely virgin boy," she said. "Swaddled in your night dress like an overgrown savior."

"Considerably overgrown," he said, "and not much good at saving."

She looked at him strangely. "Perhaps not souls. Nobody can save one's soul except oneself. But you saved the night for me." Then she grew playful. "Your hair is even more yellow than mine. It's the color of sugar birds. And as for the rest of you, even through all that cloth I can see those firm arms and legs. Do you know what, Charlie? Jill swims in the lagoon with nothing on!"

He had to admit to a momentary shock. Victorian girls who went swimming usually garbed themselves as if for Purdah, segregated themselves from men, and shut themselves from the shore with bathing machines.

"One day you will swim in the lagoon like Jill and think you're all alone, but I will slip up behind a banyan tree and blend right in with the roots and spy on you."

"You may be disappointed," he began. "I'm not as tall as I ought to be. Just middling. That's the best you can say. And I have a mole on my back shoulder, and—"

She interrupted him with a laugh. "You don't even recognize the banter of a fallen woman. Here you chatter away as if I were a respectable matron. I had rather hoped to shock you into shocking me."

He yawned and stretched like a sleepy bear. "I'm too happy to be shocked."

"And you still have your virtue," she sighed. "Really, my dear, it isn't fair. You ought to feel horribly frustrated. Instead, you've had your teacakes and eaten them too."

Morning-glories lifted purple—no, indigo—chalices around the window, but there was something wrong about them. An absence…of what?

"Why don't the birds come to your window?" he asked. "Even at Marlborough we had sparrows in the morning."

"They used to come, when Jill was a little girl. But she never liked them. She said they were cruel and spiteful and we only thought them pretty because of their feathers, which were like a cloak to hide their ugly hearts. She began to throw rocks at them. One day she took some oleander juice—you know, it's quite deadly—and sprinkled it over the morning-glories. The birds that came that morning were all poisoned. None of them come any more, not even the little sugar birds which are everywhere else on the island."

"What a horrible thing for Jill to do!"

"It was Curk who thought of the poison."

"Curk?"

"My manager. You saw him the afternoon you arrived."

"Yes, I saw him. He lives in the house with the cannons, doesn't he?"

"Yes. He visits with Jill sometimes. Teaches her things."

"I think he's a bad teacher"

"But of course he is. That's why I sent for you."

"Then I'm going to try to keep her away from him."

"That may be difficult. Do you know what his people call him?"

"No."

CHAPTER SIX

Jill was staring down the crater as if she would like to be visiting with the Caribs instead of studying in Rouaulls's *French Grammar.* But Charlie had already made far too many concessions to her. They would study not in the library, she had insisted, amidst a resplendent collection of world classics bound in leather, but under the cassia trees. They would sit on a particularly knobby area of ground, which Jill seemed to find as comfortable as moss though Charlie would have preferred a bench or an expanse of soft leaves. She was wearing her usual shortened sailor togs—he had never seen her in a gown—and he himself was garbed in a larger outfit of bell-bottom trousers, unshortened, but otherwise similar, jacket, scarf, and round, flat cap.

He did not object to looking like a sailor, and he knew that small concessions were necessary if he was to win large ones from her, and at least achieve a tentative truce between them and lessen her appalling ignorance on most subjects to be found in books. Only her knowledge about the flora and fauna of the Caribbean seemed extensive. Today he had listened for fifteen minutes to a lecture about the predatory fish in the seas around Oleandra ("not only sharks but barracudas, small but moody and you ought to see their teeth!") and then he had insisted on the French.

But she stared down the hill.

"Miss Meynell, you may join your friends after we have covered six more verbs. So far we have covered two, and I think you have already forgotten them." Today, as always, he was quite alone in making demands of her. Mrs. Meynell was resting and not to be disturbed. The household staff, that is the old man and his muffled little son, avoided Jill as if she had typhoid fever, perhaps because she consorted with the Caribs, whom they looked upon as unmitigated savages.

"Mr. Sorley, I am not in the least interested in your irregular verbs. I've decided they're unnecessary for conversing with the sailors on the boats from Martinique." Except in moments of anger, her speech, unlike her dress, was correct and curiously formal; she appeared to have learned rhetoric from her mother. "I can understand them already, and they don't worry about tenses." That morning Mrs. Meynell had insisted that she submit to a prolonged hair brushing, and she looked almost like a girl, with a hint of prettiness which with years and cultivation could blossom into her mother's beauty. It was significant, though, that whenever Charlie thought of her looks, it was in terms of how she approached or fell short of her mother.

"Your mother has expressly asked me to teach you French. Do you want to disappoint her?" He knew that he sounded insufferable. There was something about being a tutor which made one act tutorial, superior, condescending.

"My mother is a beautiful woman with a spectacular bosom, as I've noticed you noticing. All the men do. No, I don't want to disappoint her. But I would rather speak Carib than French."

The observation about bosoms was unthinkable for a Victorian girl of fifteen, who was expected to refer to the leg of a piano as a "limb" and to pretend that her bosom did not exist, even though when she reached womanhood she was allowed to flaunt it provocatively at the opera or the theatre and men were allowed to stare shamelessly so long as they pretended to be admiring a ruffle or a pendant. Charlie had never heard such frankness from a girl. But it was the truth of her observation rather than the frankness which stung him.

He slammed shut the book and shoved it into Jill's hand. "Study it or throw it in the lagoon, for all I care. I'm going for a walk."

"You were engaged to be my tutor."

"And you refuse to be tutored."

"Why don't you tutor me in history? I love battles, especially the bloody ones. Did you know that more than two-thirds of the men died in the Charge of the Light Brigade, and the whole thing was a mistake?"

If she was going to discuss battles, he could at least introduce her to some of the Laureate's poetry, even his inferior poems.

"Into the valley of death
Rode the six hundred..."

"That's one poem I already know," she interrupted. "Thanks to Mother. I would just as soon study French as listen to Tennyson. He never fought in a battle. There's no gore in the poem."

"I'll see you at supper." He strode through the cassia trees and began his descent to the lagoon. At last he was coming for our daily visit! I caught sight of him as he emerged from the English village, and I made a double somersault in the air. Mrs. Meynell had told him that he was to have as much time to himself as he chose ("Jill is too trying for constant companionship") and by this time, the end of his first week on the island, our visits had become regular and, at least on my part, anticipated with more pleasure than a school of slow-swimming mullets.

Only with me could he admit his loneliness. Only with me could he talk about his brother and his mother or describe his baffling confrontations with Jill, each of them, he felt, a resounding failure. Stripping off his shirt (and everything else when we swam to the far side of the lagoon), he would wade into the water and start, "I know you can't understand me, but..." and I would snort, "Oh, but I can," and then he would tell me the events which you are now hearing in my history, or he would rehearse a lesson in French or literature which he would later repeat to Jill. The frustration of our visits was that he had no idea I could understand him (I could even understand his French). Why would he not let me tutor him in my own language? From our several meetings, all he had learned was my name "Gloomer," which I had endlessly repeated in as human a fashion as I could manage through an air-hole. As for his name, I could not enunciate the *"Ch."* *"Arlie"* was as close as I could come, and he did not appear to recognize my approximation.

It is a human vanity to assume that every animal exists to be eaten, trapped, or taught, and even perceptive Charlie, though he did none of these things to me, did not guess that perhaps some animals could teach some humans. All he knew was that some animals could eat some humans. Delphinese is not as difficult as English or French. It is rich in verbs (without tenses) and nouns (without declensions), but lacks articles and minimizes prepositions. It is imagistic, picture-making, suggestive, rather than direct and logical. Dolphins from the seas around Japan say that it resembles Japanese, though it is much less difficult.

"So you see," he was ending, "I'm at a total loss as to how to reach that girl."

Materializing with her usual suddenness, Jill stalked onto the beach in time to hear his last sentence. I turned a frantic cartwheel to alert him but succeeded only in fixing his attention all the more intently on me. He laughed at what seemed to him my antics.

"Gloomer, you can always make me forget my troubles."

Plop!

The stone landed just beside my head and I streaked frantically for deep waters and only paused to turn and look when I was beyond the range of her powerful throwing arm. What I saw delighted me.

With infinite and unhurried dignity, Charlie waded ashore and confronted the culprit. At the same time, with the corner of his eyes he cast about for a piece of driftwood. Perhaps she thought that he meant to throw the wood for me to catch; certainly she did not anticipate his intentions toward her, the young mistress of the manor, until he loomed above her (not very tall, to be sure, but with an illusion of tallness—no, immensity) and, quick as a mongoose, snapped her over his knee and began to cane her with the driftwood. She screeched, she swore in English, French, and Carib, she struggled to kick or bite him, and she was a very strong, even though skinny young girl. But she landed not a single blow or bite; she did not even break the rhythmic descent of the makeshift cane. It was not hard wood, and they were not hard blows; she would sustain no bruises except to her pride. But her very helplessness infuriated her more than physical pain.

When he had finished he stood up and tossed her out of his lap. She tumbled onto her knees. "And if you ever throw a rock at my friend again, you'll get worse than a caning," he said.

She sat, woeful and defeated, on the hot black sand of the beach; her eyes were red and her lips were quivering. But she was not so much hurt and angry as dumbfounded by his boldness.

Feeling secure after Charlie's triumph, I swam within easier listening distance.

"Are you going to behave?" he demanded.

Her answer was scarcely audible. "Yes."

"You won't throw any more stones at Gloomer?"

"Not unless be tries to hurt me."

He held out his hand and lifted her to her feet. "He won't try to hurt you."

"But I told you what dolphins are like," she insisted. "They deserve to have rocks thrown at them. If you keep on swimming with the one out there, he'll surprise you some day and ram you the way he does a shark."

"Nonsense. He's the only friend I have on the island besides your mother. You have a terribly warped notion about dolphins. You must have gotten it from the Caribs."

All she could say was, "Anything that ugly has to be wicked." (Do you wonder that I disliked her? True, I was a little plump, but ugly? Why not bountiful like Mrs. Meynell or, since I was a male, stocky? Actually, I was losing weight; I was so happy in Charlie's company that I no longer found it necessary to gorge my grief.)

"It depends on the way you look at him. To me, he's quite beautiful. Look at the grace in those lines. And the smoothness of his skin."

She no longer tried to argue with him. Something had changed in their relationship. She had not really understood, I think, why he had punished her for throwing a rock at what seemed to her a cruel and hideous animal, but he had asserted his maleness, his mastery, he had overpowered her, and what is more, she could hardly ignore the splendor of his bare chest, still glistening from the lagoon, the wet trousers clinging to his thighs, the sunburst of his hair. He was no longer beneath contempt. He was worth, if not her understanding as yet, at least her fascination. It frightened me to see the change. So long as they were open enemies, he would be on guard. But if they began to like each other, he would become vulnerable to her caprices, her latent femininity, and to something far more insidious: whatever it was which gave her such power on the island; over the English servants, the Caribs, and her mother.

"I will study the French now," she said.

"After I've had my swim." He waded into the water and for a full half hour, while Jill waited with surprising patience, we streaked over the lagoon. For skimming the surface, he held loosely to my dorsal fin just as I had taught him, but by now he had learned to leap simultaneously with me from the water: he could tell from a sudden burst of speed that I planned a leap, and then as I rose under him he would grasp my body and fling himself upward in unison with me to lessen my burden, and we would break into the air like a single creature. We must have resembled a Triton to those on shore, body of man, tail of fish, showering drops beneath us like a tiny thunder squall. I lost no chance to show Jill that, even if I was a trifle stocky, she would never see a swifter and more agile dolphin, and I positively flaunted my friendship with Charlie. When he finally released my fin and gave me a parting hug, I swam after him, caught his ankle between my jaws, and tried to hold him for another swim. But he looked over his shoulder with mild reproof (he was never really cross with me) and I reluctantly loosed him to join the girl.

"You just won't be warned," she said to him on the beach.

"About Gloomer?" How sweet my name sounded on his lips, though his pronunciation lacked that whistling intonation which it possessed in Delphinese. "Come in the water one day and I'll show you how safe he is."

(Just let her try! I would restrain myself from ramming, but she would get the nip of her life.)

She shuddered. "I would just as soon be in a room with a bird. And I detest birds."

"You're afraid they would get in your hair?"

"I don't even like them outdoors. They're so cruel and garish."

"But you have the loveliest birds I ever saw here on Oleandra. All those bright colors. The trogon with its green and rose—"

She pointed to the black sand. "That's my favorite color."

"Then you ought to like Gloomer."

"He isn't really black. Dirty gray on top. Dirty white on the bottom. And anyway, it isn't his color I don't like. It's his character."

"You'll get to like him. I'll see to that. Now for some French."

"Yes. Only…"

"Only what, Miss Meynell?"

"I waited half an hour for you. Don't you owe me a favor?"

"No, but you can ask for one."

"I want to show you my tree house. My own house. Nobody else goes there except Curk. It isn't far from here and you'll have a chance to dry off before we go back to the Red House."

"I would like that," he said, with more kindness than I liked. I knew about boys of nineteen. Show them a girl, even in pants, and though they begin as enemies, the next thing you know there are whispers and nuzzlings and secret trysts. We have the same foolishness among dolphins. After all, Charlie was only four years older than Jill. Sometimes she looked like a little girl, but now there was something disquietingly adult about her. The spanking had worked an unfortunate, if hopefully short-lived, miracle. One of these days, however, she would sprout a real bosom, and then might the Great Triton help Charlie!

He anticipated a tree house lodged among leafy branches, with a ladder of woven rushes to be raised or lowered at will to invite guests or escape enemies, and a little room with a downy floor and a collection of prized objects saved from childhood: sea-shells, toys, perhaps even a book about life in the sea or famous battles. He was thinking of the tree house he and his brother Kenneth had built when they were twelve (their book had been Kingsley's *Water Babies)*. Furthermore, after his dip with me, he was not in the least eager for French grammar, which bored him almost as much as it did Jill.

"Lead the way," he said, trying to sound as if he were doing her a favor. For the sake of his position, he could not capitulate too readily. He looked back at me with real regret. "I wish Gloomer could go with us. How would you like to be trapped all your life in the water?"

"I expect he thinks *we're* trapped, don't you?" ("No," I snorted. "I'd much prefer the land.")

"I think he's lucky myself. If you'd ever swum with Curk, you'd know it was, well, like the Carib notion of paradise. All those sea-caves where the only light is noctiluca or phosphorus. The forests of seaweed right on the ocean floor. Have you ever seen an octopus under water? As Curk says, they don't swim, they flow. There's nothing more beautiful than watching their eight legs making a little river behind them." There was that name again, the cryptic Curk. I desperately wanted

Charlie to ask her about him, but she gave him no chance. She took his hand and pulled him away from the beach and out of my sight. I have rarely hated so much to see him leave because I knew—knew that there was something unpleasant in store for him. When Jill was hateful, she was at least predictable; she threw stones. When she was happy, who could predict her behavior?

The tree house was not lodged among the blossoms of a shower-of-gold or fragrantly entwined with the boughs of a frangipani. It was hidden in the heart of that arboreal freak, the banyan tree, whose slender trunk flares into branches which send down countless feelers that not only dip to touch the earth, but grow into the earth (or are they roots growing out of the earth?), so that you feel the one tree is a whole little forest. It is a curious, even an interesting tree, but full of shifting shadows and almost sinister. It might be likened to a forest of immense sea anemones. Dolphins avoid such forests because they conceal giant squids and moray eels.

"But where is the house?" Charlie asked "All I see are branches."

With true pride of ownership, she led him into the network, sidestepping, circling, climbing over a branch which grew along the ground like a snake before piercing the earth.

"Here," she said. She brushed aside a carpet of leaves and pointed to a trapdoor, a square of banyan wood with a brass, piratical-looking handle. "Here's my house." They climbed down a ladder, not the charming gossamer one of rushes which Charlie had fancied, but crooked and jagged and cut down the side of a big root, and found themselves in a chamber so dark that Charlie could not even tell its dimensions.

"I love the dark," said Jill. "Listen. You can hear my friends."

He could hear an ominous rustling over dry leaves. "Haven't you a lamp?" he asked a bit nervously. Even stout

English schoolboys are afraid of snakes in the dark on a strange island.

"I can see in the dark," she said.

"I can't see a thing except the square of light around the trapdoor."

"Very well then. I don't want you to miss anything." She busied herself invisibly in the dark for what seemed to Charlie long enough for both of them to be bitten by snakes, and finally lit a paraffin lamp.

He blinked to assure himself that the dim light was not deceiving him.

"But it's a tomb," he cried at last. "There're skeletons all over the place."

"You talk as if they were just strewn about," she reproved him. "They are laid to rest, and there is a great difference. You're right, though, this used to be a Carib burial vault, but there's something so tranquil and sacred about it. You're in the midst of death and you see how beautiful it is. And look at my friends, how happy they are here!"

She knelt and touched her hand to a skeleton and a huge tarantula climbed leg over hairy leg up her arm. The legs looked sinewy even beneath the hair. He knew the jumping power of those furry beasts.

"The light frightens them. You have to make them feel at ease."

"They're quite deadly, aren't they?" he said in what emerged as a whisper.

"Little worse than a bee sting. Unless of course a lot of them bite you. And they do tear the skin. But they know their friends."

"Are there many of them down here?"

"Ten adults and thirty or so babies. It's hard to keep track of the young."

He slapped at a tickle on his wrist and, without looking, was sure that he had reduced the young to twenty-nine. He was glad that she did not keep exact count. Already he was groping for the ladder.

"Where are you going?" she demanded. "You're with me. They won't hurt you."

"They may not recognize me as a friend."

Silently she followed him up the ladder, and they stood together outside the banyan tree looking at each other with that total failure of communication which is all the more painful because both persons have genuinely tried to communicate. He knew that she had brought him here in good faith, that she had not expected to endanger or frighten him. It was her first real gesture of friendship. But the room to him had seemed worse than frightening; it had seemed hideous. He looked at his trousers to make sure that no tarantula had ridden him down the ladder.

Her lips were quivering. He had never seen tears on her cheeks, but he could tell that she wanted to cry. "You didn't like my house," she said. It was not an accusation so much as an expression of despair.

"It wasn't what I expected. It was so dark, and then the spiders—"

"But they're beautiful. I can watch them for hours. All that black glossy fur like a wolf. I never saw a real wolf but I have a picture of one in a geography book. And the green eyes. Of course, it was too dark for you to see the eyes down there, but you ought to look at them in the daylight."

"But the skeletons. Don't you feel uncomfortable with them lying all around you?"

"Oh, no, those were Carib kings and queens you saw. They were laid out in state, and they still wear aquamarine pendants around their necks to ward off evil spirits. I wish I could be buried there. I wish I were a Carib too! Not like the ones you see on Oleandra. I love them, but they're weak and degenerate, bad little children who have to be made to mind. Curk himself says so. But they were a great people before

Columbus came and the Spaniards started stealing their lands. You can see what they were like from Curk."

"What's wrong with being English? Your mother is a charming woman."

She paused and said thoughtfully, "I love my mother. I really do. But I don't respect her. She's soft. She's always being sick and going to bed. It's only Curk who keeps the Caribs working for her. Without him, they'd strip the house and pack her off to Martinique on the next boat. Or worse."

"Curk. The Man Who Swims with the Sharks. He must be very brave."

"Yes!" Her eyes glowed greenly like those of the tarantulas she had described. Not with evil, but simply without goodness. Unconcerned with laws and customs. Whether the expression belonged to her or the man she was reflecting, it was hard to say; perhaps to both. "He's the bravest man in the world. The last of the Carib kings. You saw him when you first came to the Red House."

"I caught just a glimpse of him. He was the one who ordered the carriers away, wasn't he?"

"Yes. You'll see a lot more of him. This is his island, and it was his idea to—"

"To what, Jill?" For the first time, he had used her given name.

"To bring you here. It wasn't my idea. I didn't want anyone except Curk. That's why I was so hateful to you at first. But he said I needed you. And then, on the beach a little while ago, I thought—I thought maybe he was right. You were like him for a while. You hurt me so beautifully. I didn't know, at first, that it was because I had thrown a rock at that stupid dolphin. But you were your own law, and that was enough. But now I just don't know."

Charlie was incredulous. "It was his idea for you to have a tutor?"

"That was the excuse he gave Mother. He knew she really did want me taught. How to be a lady. How to enjoy

THE GOAT WITHOUT HORNS | 77

poetry. How to speak French. And she wanted company. So he encouraged her to write Mr. Lane. She asked for a poet-type, and a good looking one at that. But Curk put in the part about the sciences. He taught himself to read and write, you know. He respects knowledge immensely, though his own reading has been mostly in the Bible—he can recite the Book of Kings word for word. And he insisted on your being a fine athlete. Mother didn't know what he really had in mind. Or if she knew, she pretended not to, because she felt she shouldn't approve of such a thing. She's good at closing her eyes. Like a stork."

"An ostrich."

"That's it. Ostrich. It's the stork that brings the babies in those stupid children's books. Mother's an ostrich. So you see you had to be all kinds of things to us. A poet for Mother. An athlete for Curk and to make the Caribs respect you. And virile because—" She began to stammer. She groped for the words which usually spilled from her tongue like petals from a shower-of-gold tree or, depending on her mood, like venom from the fangs of a fer-de-lance.

He said, with the desperation of dawning knowledge, "I still don't know what you're trying to tell me."

"—Because you must give me strong children."

CHAPTER SEVEN

He had brought her to the beach by means of a path which tumbled like a stream down the craterside, veering, swooping, narrowing between lemon and calamondin trees and expanding onto terraces green with cacao plants. At the end of the path he had to lift her from the burro and support her to the edge of the water.

I had watched his descent from the lagoon, and my dorsal fin had stiffened with pride, almost like a plume, because they were coming to see *me*.

"And this," he said proudly, "is Gloomer."

In spite of evident fatigue, Mrs. Meynell was fully as beautiful as Charlie had led me to anticipate. She was wearing a croquet dress, one of those gowns which English ladies don for the out-of-doors but which is quite as voluminous as a ball gown. The difference lay in the material and design. Her attire was an inexpensive muslin with a polka-dotted skirt and blouse of vertical stripes, and a little black ribbon at her throat and a hat so tiny that it might have been a rose perched in her golden garden of backswept hair. It was the late afternoon, and her parasol, which was like a larger rosebud and more decorative than practical, had not been necessary to shield her from the sun. She reminded me of a garden: the frangipani scent of her, the marigold hair and the camellia lips, even the lily pallor of her cheeks. "There is a garden in her face," Charlie was fond of quoting.

He himself had walked, leading both Mrs. Meynell's burro and a pack animal laden with cushions, coverlets, and viands for a picnic. He began to make her a nest under a carob tree which grew close to the water. But she insisted first on standing and visiting with me. Her mysterious malady which caused her reluctance to leave her bed she had never identified, and

Charlie had always ascribed it to her dependence on laudanum. I suspected a more sinister explanation. At any rate, she was never totally bed-ridden.

I had swum so close to shore that I was in real danger of floundering on the sand. But I knew that Charlie would hasten to my rescue and drag me, tail first, into deep waters. I wriggled along the bottom like a sting-ray for the closest possible view of her.

You know how critical I am of new acquaintances, but Charlie had predisposed me in her favor, and when I found that he had not exaggerated, I lost my heart to her. Such a lush and soft-curving creature! Such a generosity of bosom! It was hard to realize that weedy Jill had been spawned by this voluptuous Amphitrite.

What is more, she was not condescending to me. "Gloomer," she said, as if she knew that I could understand her, (which of course I could), "Charlie has told me about his friend in the lagoon, and I want to tell you how honored I am to pay you a visit. I often watch you from my window and you're the most beautiful swimmer I've ever seen. I'm glad Charlie has such a friend." (If she watched me, she must also watch Charlie. Really, he ought to wear a bathing suit!)

By this time Charlie had completed the nest under the carob tree, swept the ground clean of pods, arranged a pillow and coverlet; but all the while he had been watching Mrs. Meynell and me out of the corner of his eye and judging how well his friends liked each other. Our amenities exchanged and our friendship established, he settled Mrs. Meynell against the tree, a cushion at her back, and poured her a cup of punch: rum and fruit juices, lime, papaya, and pineapple, mixed to a liquid ambrosia, from a silver flagon with a head like that of a greyhound. While Charlie walked to the edge of the water to greet me, she drank the punch with the avidity of a mariner rescued from a raft in a tropical sun. Charlie unwrapped a parcel and drew out a large decapitated mullet (of course, we never eat their heads; that would be barbarous) which he presented to me as if I were the third member of the picnic. I took it from his fingers and crunched and swallowed it with grateful zest. Returning to the carob tree, he prepared to pour himself some punch, but Mrs. Meynell blandly held out her cup, which he refilled with some surprise. Being none too fastidious in my own gastronomical habits (except when it comes to mullet heads), I could sympathize with her. Ladies were expected to sip their beverages but Mrs. Meynell had every right to gulp after so taxing a journey.

The mullet was settling into my second stomach when a loud, reproving voice disturbed my digestion and my daydreams. Jill approached the tree with the bad temper of an excluded guest. She and Charlie had not met since she had confessed the reason why Curk had brought him to the island. They had carefully avoided each other and now she appeared to have worked herself into a rage.

"Mother will be sick all night from this outing you've dragged her on," she snapped. "Are you my tutor or her self-appointed physician?"

"I asked Charlie to bring me," Mrs. Meynell replied with some asperity. "Here, Jill, join us under the tree."

"I haven't any appetite," she said. "That creature in the water turns my stomach. He's watching every move we make. It's as if, as if he were trying to be one of us."

"He is one of us," Charlie said,

"Then I'm not." She flounced up the trail toward the house.

Charlie looked after her with the anger he justifiably felt on behalf of an insulted friend

"Never mind," I wanted to say, did say in my usual—to him unrecognizable wheeze. "I have my friends with me. What do I care about a petulant child?"

But Jill was not a child, and her petulance was more like the anger of a rejected woman.

Charlie was exuberant. "Do you realize that this has been your most active day yet? You were out of bed three hours this afternoon."

"Three hours? Three months! My dear, I am one continuous ache. I feel as if I have been nailed in a barrel and rolled over a waterfall." She nestled gratefully into her pillows. "And half the time jostling on the back of a burro, which I haven't ridden for two years."

"It was the only way for you to get to the lagoon. You'd never have managed it on foot."

"Or without you to keep me on the burro. I don't know which of you carried more of me."

"But don't you see," Charlie expostulated, "you *had* to meet Gloomer. And he couldn't very well come to you."

"I'm glad I met him," she said, suddenly serious. "Every day I've watched you swim in the lagoon, and Gloomer has been with you."

"He's my friend."

"Never swim without him, Charlie."

"Oh, I can handle myself in the water all right. You know how many rivers we have in England."

"A river is not a lagoon. *Never swim without him.*"

The words were a commandment.

"I don't intend to. He keeps me company."

"Keeps you company? He's more than a pet, isn't he?

"Your best friend," she mused. "Of course he is. He isn't a fish at all, is he? He's a mammal, and mammals are suckled by their mothers. They learn how to love. He can be a stout friend to you in the water. But the shore, Charlie. How can he help you here?"

"Why should I need help, Elizabeth?" He spoke her given name for the first time, and without embarrassment; indeed with pleasure. Elizabeth. It was a storied name. A great queen; a beloved poet. It had a resonance as well as a history. Yes, it suited her.

"Did you know there were once Africans on this island? A slave ship was wrecked on the coast, and there must have been a hundred Negroes at one time living quite happily along these slopes."

"What happened to them?"

"The Caribs gave a great feast and invited the Africans as guests of honor. They even asked the mothers to bring their babies. Once the Africans were thoroughly drunk on fermented cassava juice, the Caribs roasted and ate them as if they were suckling pigs."

Charlie shuddered. "I knew they were cruel," he said. "The day I landed on Oleandra, one of them threw a stone at Gloomer and the others laughed. But cannibals—"

She pressed his hand. "The Caribs were notorious in their early days. But that was centuries ago. That is why they have almost been exterminated through these islands—first by the Spanish, then the English, then the Africans. You'll find a few isolated colonies—on Dominica—here on Oleandra. In most places they are no longer numerous enough to be a threat."

"But what about you and Jill? You have two servants in your house. Counting you, Jill, and me, there are only five English people on the whole island. There must be forty or more Caribs."

"Thirty. They seem more numerous than they are because they look so much alike. It's easy to count the same one twice."

"Suppose they gave a feast—"

She shook her head, "We have need of each other, the Caribs and I. Jill and I are quite safe from them, and so are you unless—unless you make someone very angry. Do you understand me, Charlie?"

"I think I do."

"And you must caution your friend Gloomer to keep out of their reach. To them, he's just another fish to be caught and eaten."

"He isn't edible," said Charlie. "The kind of dolphin you eat is a true fish and much smaller."

"Charlie, Charlie. Always the teacher. If they couldn't eat him, they would kill him just for the sport of it and feed his carcass to the seagulls."

"If they did," said Charlie brusquely, "there would be five or six fewer Caribs on the island." His voice softened. "You liked him, didn't you? I could see that at once. And he liked you."

"Jill doesn't like him, though."

"No, and I'm not sure why, except that she finds him ugly. He's never done anything to her—teased or frightened her. But he doesn't like her either. She won't go in the water when he's close by. Do you think he reminds her of a shark?"

Elizabeth looked at him fixedly before she spoke. "My daughter is not in the least afraid of sharks. I would say, rather, that she dislikes him because he does not remind her of a shark. Because dolphins and sharks are hereditary enemies. Now you must leave me, Charlie. I'm very tired."

"Because of me," he said ruefully.

"Yes, because of you. But it's a happy tiredness. Not that long, gray weariness which seems to have no cause and no conclusion. I haven't been so happy since I left England. It's been a—*Wordsworthian*—day."

"Let's say a Browningesque day. *'Oh, to be in England, now that April's there...'* You remind me of Mrs. Browning, you know. I cried all day when she died, though I was just a little child at the time."

"And you want me to rise from my bed of pain and bloom again."

"You've never ceased to bloom. It's just that you shut yourself away from everyone who might admire you. *'A violet by a mossy stone, half hidden from the eye...'* Those are the only lines by Wordsworth I like."

"My petals are wilted, I'm afraid."

"They're full-blooming."

He left her and thought with surprise and guilt: I have not been sad all day...

But he came back to her in an hour, wearing his nightdress and carrying a taper, because he was afraid that he had overtaxed her strength; that his well-meant enthusiasm had condemned her to a night of pain and sleeplessness. Really, his escapade had been inexcusable for a mature young man of nineteen. To coax an invalid from her bed and onto the back of a burro…

There was no scent of laudanum in the air. She was lying on her back with open eyes and she smiled at him without surprise.

He knelt and kissed her cheek. "You haven't taken your laudanum. Can you sleep without it?"

"I wanted to lie awake awhile and remember the day." As always a scent of frangipani hovered about her like an invisible cloak. She had combed her hair around her shoulders and, far from accenting her years, it made her appear to be ageless, blooming, eternal—a saffron Ceres, an earth mother (but no longer his own mother) who had lost her daughter but kept her beauty through uncountable winters of grief.

"I've come to say good-night."

She patted his head. "I thought you already had."

"Not in those exact words. I merely *implied* a good night."

"You were afraid you had overtaxed me?"

"Yes."

"No. No, my dear, you have given me strength of a very precious kind."

He astonished himself with his next pronouncement. "I'm going to stay with you again."

"Not tonight, Charlie. The thought of you will companion me. Your actual presence, well, it *would* overtax my strength."

"I surely won't tire you if I hold you in my arms. You may consider me an extra pillow."

She assumed an air of flippancy. "Your chest is admirable but for softness mine is superior. You would get the best of the arrangement."

"Try the crook of my shoulder. It's expressly made to cradle a head."

THE GOAT WITHOUT HORNS | 85

"You won't understand," she blurted in one of her sudden and baffling changes of mood. "The other time it was all very well for you, the charitable young man, to please a neurotic lady's whim. You could preen yourself on your sacrifice. But now your charity, as well as your chastity, is beginning to stifle me."

"You think I came out of charity?" he protested. "Not the first time and certainly not now."

"Out of loneliness then. You wanted to be mothered. But I don't feel maternal at the moment. In your night-dress you look like a good-natured banshee, but I have watched you swim in the lagoon without a stitch, and my conception of you is quite robust. I have already lost one night of sleep to your platonic endearments. I told you what I am—a loose, immoral woman—and yet you come a second time to offer me brotherhood. Save that for Gloomer."

He did not try to conceal his hurt. "We talk too much and understand too little. Sometimes I feel I know Gloomer better than any friend I have, and yet neither can understand a word the other says."

In spite of her protestations, he held her in his arms with gentleness and yet with a certain insistence which was not to be denied. He felt the rigidity ebb from her body.

In a tiny voice she said, "Stay then. But not for the night. Just for an hour or two."

"Your lips taste like flowers," he said. "And they're soft as petals. It's like touching camellias. I'm afraid I might bruise them."

"No more than a hawk moth or a butterfly. Hush. Hush now, my dear. You have just said that words confuse and deceive. We shall make—and therefore break—no promises. In a large darkness, we shall share our little light and no monsters shall frighten us."

Her invalidism excited his pity; her beauty, his desire. Dimly he recognized those weaknesses of character which had led her to mock him at times and even, in a way which he could not explain, to endanger him. He was coming to sense that Oleandra was as beautiful and poisonous as the flower for which it was named, and that Elizabeth herself had imbibed some of the poison. But now was no time for moral judgments. Now was the time to make love to her. Not to the shadowy Annabelle Lee of that other night, but to a woman of flesh and blood who in her own curious way, half maternal, half amorous, ashamed and yet proud, needed him with a longing urgency. The perfume which was her distinctive scent, distilled in part from the frangipani, seemed to speak for her, to say that in some ways she was staunch and pure like the tree. And yet the soft, at times almost cloying sweetnesses mingled with the frangipani were the faults, the evasions, the yieldings which had kept her from fullest stature. But who was he to judge her, he who had fled from England rather than face his grief? A true lover was never a judge.

He knew that he had not been wrong to preserve his chastity for such a time. He had not been wrong to resist the urges of friends who waited for harlots behind the music hall and boasted of nights in beds surrounded by mirrors and lit by a hundred tapers. Darkness was the proper state for love, because love was its own light. It glowed like a Japanese lantern, warming and illuminating; in this case, a fragile one perhaps, bamboo and paper and not wrought iron. Evanescent, perhaps, who could say? But exquisite.

He had heard from his friends—he had read in the copies of Ovid and Catullus secreted under the covers of his bed at Marlborough—that passion must be inflamed by an exchange of calculated caresses and whispered obscenities; that kisses must mount from gentleness to ferocity; embraces to a savage climax. But he took her without calculation; with an unstudied tenderness which redeemed his inexperience.

Was he better, you may ask, than his furtive, lecherous friends because in this canopied bed, he loved with splendor instead of secrecy and squalor; loved a lady instead of a harlot? Yes, a resounding yes. He could love without guilt because he did not betray his own high code. Because to Charlie the only sin in "love-making" was really "loveless-making"; the sin of estranging the heart and the body, when the body took what it wanted, exulted in fleshly conquest, while the heart looked on, a bemused and envious stranger.

To a dolphin there is no marriage and no constancy between lovers, and "love" is a word reserved for friends, parents, and children. Male and female perform in an endless play of amorous dalliance, grow fond of each other, exchange gifts of sea anemones or pink coral, but change partners with the restlessness and readiness of dancers at an English waltz. The mother adores her child, but the child's father—if indeed she knows his identity—she treats with the same light-hearted camaraderie as her other lovers. It was not so with Charlie. His heart and his body, acting in loving concert, were unestranged. He would love again; he would love more deeply perhaps; he would never love more sweetly.

His last word to her, almost the only word he spoke in all that time, was Elizabeth. It was the second time he had used her given name, an extraordinary boldness for one of his years and his position in her home as the tutor of her child, and yet he used it without presumption, without possession. She was no longer the great lady of a manor house but one who, like himself, had lit her loneliness with a lantern of love.

Drowsily ebbing into sleep, he wondered if he heard or dreamed her answer.

"Thank you, my dear. Thank you. Now you must go."

He had not believed her when she had promised him a few hours. He had expected the night. He was shocked into wakefulness.

"Because—?"

"Of him."

CHAPTER EIGHT

The next morning, Jill had intercepted him on his way to the lagoon. His thoughts, during and after a sleepless night, had been of Elizabeth and the Man Who Swam with the Sharks. They were not pleasant thoughts; Charlie was jealous, blindly and helplessly jealous for the first time in his life. But Jill had looked so chastened that he had stopped to talk to her.

She had not stopped him to talk.

"Curk wants us," she had said, and he had followed her not unwillingly to her banyan tree, for he wished at last to confront this Carib, this king, this rival who loomed so fearsomely between him and Elizabeth…

He was a man who appeared to be about forty, thought Charlie, and then at once he began to amend his impression. God, not man, was the word, but one of those elemental Aztec gods who sent showers to the parching fields only after they had been propitiated by the sacrifice of a thousand captives. He was beyond man's law because he was beyond man; both more and less. Lordly in strength, but no more compassionate than a waterspout.

And his age? Forty was too precise. As with Mrs. Meynell there were no lines to mark the passage of years, griefs, triumphs, defeats. His hair, combed long behind his head and braided around the bone of an animal, was thick, glossy, and black as the sharks with which he was said to swim. Aquamarine pendants hung from his pierced ears and the deep incisions cut in his cheeks were outlined and darkened with coal; he was savage, but not a savage. A keen intelligence, analyzing, evaluating, glittered in his eyes. He was not a god Charlie could worship; nor a man he could judge, like, despise, or even comprehend.

Charlie stood beneath his immensity without cowering, met his gaze without blinking, but feared him as he had feared no other man. Inscrutable, unsmiling, neither dispensing nor denying his favor, Curk had emerged from the shower-of-gold trees, thrusting aside a branch which barred his path and scattering the petals like a whirlwind.

Jill advanced to meet him. She smiled and started to speak his name.

He stopped her with a raised hand. "It is almost time for the Goat Without Horns."

She was not affronted by his rebuff. He whom she worshipped had withheld his smile but what he had told her explained his solemnity.

Fear and eagerness mingled in her face and made her, in one of her startling shifts of mood, more woman than child. At that moment she was as unknowable as Curk. She seized Charlie's hand and drew him beside her onto the ground. He did not have to be told that he should bow his head.

He saw the bare brown feet of the man who loomed above them. Long and narrow, with pointed toes and toenails trimmed like sharp little knives. He felt his warmth. His nostrils caught an overpowering scent of musk, almost like that of the male deer which wishes to attract a female, and also, infuriatingly, a hint of frangipani, as if he had come from Elizabeth's arms.

When he spoke, his voice was deep and resonant with at moments a veiled tenderness. It was a voice like muffled thunder.

"It is almost time for the Goat Without Horns," he repeated.

"Truly, Curk?"

"You know what you must do, my daughter. Are you prepared?"

"Yes, my father."

Curk placed a hand on either head: "I, Carib king to Carib princess, pronounce you mate of the Englishman. Obey him as becomes a woman, but command him as becomes a princess. May you flourish in the favor of the Omnipotent Tark and restore our people to their ancient glory."

Then he was gone, bruising the petals with silent feet.

It was Jill who broke the silence, who began to command him as became a Carib princess. With peremptory hands she raised him to his feet. She caught his head between her palms and kissed him on the mouth and said in a voice which no longer faltered, "Our differences don't matter. Curk has joined us together. You are to make love to me. You will father my children and the Carib kings will live through us."

Awe had left him along with the awful presence. Englishmen, even modest ones like Charlie, are used to governing empires. The Caribbean was almost an English sea. Anger flared in him. Who was a Carib chieftain with slit cheeks and braided hair to tell him he was married to his child—no, not married, mated? And who was the child to tell him that he must give her children—she whom he had disliked, then pitied, but hardly loved, or even thought of loving?

He fought down his anger even as he spoke. "You don't even know what you're talking about when you tell me to make love to you. Jill, you're fifteen years old. Not yet a woman. And if you were, I must still make my own choice."

She looked at him without comprehension. "But Curk has joined us. Curk, my *father*. Don't you understand?"

"No, I don't understand. I thought your father was an English adventurer."

She shrugged with contempt. "Did you expect my mother to tell you that she betrayed my father? Oh, don't look so shocked. She should have betrayed him. He was a weakling. But English ladies are reticent about such matters. And I do know how to make love. I've seen the Carib couples in the mangrove swamp and how they embrace and writhe and become one with each other. A Carib boy chased me only last year, and I wanted to stop for him, but I fled because it was for Curk to choose my lover."

Now it was Charlie who clasped her shoulders and reasserted his mastery. "Jill, I came here to be your tutor. I want to be your friend. That's all. I don't care what your father says. You love him because he's strong. Do you want me to be less strong? To do what I'm told and not what I must? You said you first liked me because I made my own law when I punished you. Surely I can break somebody else's law imposed on me against my will."

She lowered her head. "I'm so confused. It was simple before you came to the island. When I heard you were coming, and why, I was furious. But I was curious too. And then I saw you in the lagoon that first time and how beautifully you swam with that ugly animal, and how—how good you looked without any clothes, all muscle and sinew like Curk. And after you punished me, even after you didn't like my tree house, I wanted you. Besides, everybody obeys Curk. I thought you would too. I thought you would want to." She stared at him with unsettling candor. "Is it my mother you love? Curk does. She's the only soft thing he loves."

He parried the question with indignation. "Do I have to love anybody right now?"

"But don't you at least desire my body?" She was beginning to sound like a girl in a French novel, the source no doubt of her information concerning "love" and "desire." But he was far from laughing at her.

"Not yet. Perhaps in a few years. But even then no one can order me to desire you. I must be my own master. I must be like Curk in that respect."

She was crying now; crying anguishedly with all the imprisoned tears of her thwarted childhood, of a little girl who had grown up with a father whose god was strength and to whom beauty was the sweep of a shark instead of a sea-gull. She was like the living figures the Greek had believed to be imprisoned in stone. Pygmalion had not created Galatea; he had released her from her marble cage. He, Charlie, the unwilling sculptor, had struck a telling blow with his chisel, and a face stared forth from the marble. The cage was cracked but not yet broken.

He knelt beside her and laid a hand on her head. He had always been unselfconscious with his hands, his movements; one who touched as well as spoke his affection. He did not stop to think that his touch might now be a cruelty instead of a solace because it was one of pity instead of love.

"Jill, how can I help you?"

"By making love to me."

"But you don't really love me. You couldn't, in so short a time. And you said yourself how different we are."

"But I don't have to love you. Not in the way you mean. Or Mother means. Quoting poems from Tennyson and exchanging flowers. Flowers wilt anyway. What are they supposed to symbolize? Curk said we must make love, and that's not the same thing as loving, is it? I want you and that's enough."

"No, it isn't enough."

"And anyway," she blurted, "I think I do love you. I like to look at you. I like to feel your hand on my head. Even if I don't understand you. I wasn't angry when you didn't like my tree house and my friends. I was sorry for you. I wanted to teach you not to be afraid. Isn't that a kind of loving?"

"That's friendship, Jill. It might become love. But not for a long time." He was all tenderness with her now; he wanted to salve her pride, soothe her heart, stop her tears—but without encouraging her to expect his love. "Jill, I'm going to leave Oleandra. The boat from Martinique will come in a few weeks. I'm going back to England." A shower-of-gold tree arched above their heads, its gilt, acorn-shaped buds mingling with its full and falling blossoms; a cornucopia perpetually spilling abundance toward the earth. He would break a spray from the tree and place it in her hand. He would leave her this token of his deep and growing esteem. But even as he lifted her hand he thought how she hated bright colors, poems, flowers which wilted.

A tiny fiddler crab zigzagged over the ground near his feet, an ugly animal, with a claw too big for its spindly body. Somehow it had wandered too far from the lagoon and the weight of its claw made its passage a slow and meandering one. He caught it carefully so that it could not bite him and held it out to Jill.

She took it with a cry of pleasure, not by its claw but its entire body, and cradled it in her palm as he might have cradled a small bird. The claw snapped once and then subsided as the little animal seemed to be eased of its fear.

He turned to leave her.

"Charlie," she cried after him. "You called me a little girl, but I am a Carib princess. And you're rejecting me? Once and for all?"

"Once. For all, only the years can say." He felt that the years would deepen his friendship for her, but make no essential change in its nature. But he could not leave her without hope.

"If Curk knew, he would never let you leave the island. He would kill you, I think, to save my honor. I won't tell him that you didn't make love to me. Or that you're going to try to leave. It will be our secret. The only secret I've ever kept from him."

"Thank you, Jill."

"I don't want to deceive him. But I don't want him to hurt you either. When the boat comes, he mustn't know you're going on board. You can't get the Caribs to row you out in their dugouts and you can't row yourself alone. You will have to swim, but the current is very strong, to say nothing of the sharks. You must get your dolphin to help you. And Charlie—"

"Yes, Jill?"

"We shall have to pretend that we have made love. You know how a man and a woman look at each other afterwards? Touch each other sometimes with their hands and sometimes only with their eyes?" She put her arms around him and kissed him and he tasted the salt from her tears and wished for both of their sakes that he could love her; he who had never loved without being loved in return but could guess the pain because he had lost those who had loved him.

"Now I'm going into my tree house. Curk will think we're there together. He's gone to the mangrove swamp." She stopped and tenderly placed the fiddler on the ground and pointed him in the direction of the lagoon. "I can't take him into my house. They need water and light. But he was a lovely gift."

Charlie sat, head in hands, elbows on knees, in the great settle of the living room. The pain he was causing Jill and the necessity for him to leave her, and her island, wracked him with a two-fold pain. It was not that he fancied her hopelessly in love with him. He had never comprehended his own beauty; he had never thought of himself as an irresistible Lord Byron, whose smiles were an invitation, whose touch was a conquest. Jill had quite astonished him by speaking of love, and he stoutly believed that her pride and not her heart was the more wounded. Her girlish fancy had made him an object of love. It could as easily unmake him, once he had left the island.

But he had made her betray Curk, who was both her father and her god. He had made her violate her own harsh but somehow admirable integrity. It pained him to pain her, and yet if she did not help him to deceive Curk, his escape was impossible. The consequences of his deception—of his pretending to have made love to a girl whom he had not so much as kissed—he could not foresee. Curk had said that it was almost time for the Goat Without Horns. Meaningless words to Charlie. Electrifying words to Jill.

And here he sat, islanded in the Red House from the horrors of the larger island, comforted by the sheer Englishness of the architecture which he had once found depressingly bland, and by his nearness to his only understanding human friend this side of England.

Elizabeth came into the room with only the scent of frangipani to announce her presence. She walked so silently that even her voluminous skirt failed to rustle. This particular skirt was dusky blue, with a multitude of silver stars in clusters like Milky Ways. *"She walks in beauty like the night of cloudless climes and starry skies..."* Her eyes were remote with the remnants of sleep. He looked up at her with silent pleading. She sank beside him on the tall-backed settle, where Arthurian knights, subdued in color but vivid with action, jousted above their heads.

"You're troubled about Jill?" Her drowsiness vanished as soon as she saw his pain. The warmth and sweetness of her, the inexpressible comfort of one who so resembled his mother as she had looked when he was a small child, sent tears coursing down his cheeks. A young man crying can be a ridiculous sight. But Charlie's tears were not effeminate. They were not the facile tears of a coward or a crybaby, but the natural, manly expression of a grief beyond words.

"Yes."

"She's still hard and antagonistic?"

"Oh, Elizabeth, it's much worse than that. She thinks she's married to me! Curk came out of the trees and placed his hands on our heads and spoke a few words and then Jill said we were to bear his grandchildren. Is he really her father?"

She did not seem particularly surprised by Jill's behavior and she did not try to evade a question whose answer would convict her of adultery.

"Yes, my dear, he is really her father. You see I am truly a bad woman, just as I warned you. No, not bad. Weak. I loved Curk once. He still compels me with his sheer physical presence, though I know him to be—heartless. You've seen him yourself. You can imagine what he must have seemed to me when we first met. He glittered with barbaric splendor. You men like every woman to be a saint or a harlot. It so simplifies your treatment of us. The pedestal or the brothel. But most of us are mixed of sky and clay. There is something about us which yearns toward a handsome savage. We hope to tame him and at the same time hope to be mastered by him. It's no longer thought proper to admire wicked Lord Byron, but every woman I know has a copy of his poems which she hides from her husband. My own husband was a weakling, querulous and drunken, an aimless wanderer who was always sailing from places instead of to them. He had cut a handsome figure as a young man, and I had married him not unwillingly at my parents' urging. But he was as hollow as a suit of armor. I think he only liked Oleandra because at first I disliked it so intensely. We used to come ashore from our yacht and he would bring gifts to the Caribs in return for the heady rum they brewed for their festivals.

"'One day we'll settle here,'" he used to taunt me, "'and these shall be your guests as well as your servants.'

"And then I met Curk, who was strong where his countrymen and my own husband were weak, and I gave myself to him in a frenzy of love without tenderness or guilt. One year later my husband died and I, who had nothing in England except my husband's fortune—no surviving family and few friends after our years of wandering—returned to Oleandra because of Curk. Then it was known as Shark Island. I changed the name to sound like the loveliest of flowers. I imported workers and material from England and built the Red House and the cottages for my servants. And for the Caribs if they would only use them, but they preferred to stay in the mangrove swamp and dream in the sun or torture their dogs. And I have lived here all these years, lonely beyond words, yet loving— no, desiring—a man who had no knowledge of kindness, who came to me only because I was an Englishwoman and my beauty somehow attracted him. He said that I was the one star he would allow in the blackness of his chosen night. And because I could give him a child. Oh, he had fathered children on many a Carib maiden, I had no doubt of that. He was not a man to sleep alone. But he wanted my child, a child half English. 'My race is degenerate,' he used to say. 'I am its only strength. Yours is the power of England and the world. You must give me a son who is worthy of an empire.'

"I gave him Jill and never recovered my health. I fell prey to fevers of mind and body and became as you see me now, bed-ridden much of the time, melancholy all of the time, denied even the company of my daughter. For Curk took to her as soon as he found that I could bear him no more children. He treated her like the son I had failed to give him. Her dress, her hair, her manners. How little I was allowed to teach her! When Curk himself suggested a tutor from England, I wrote to Mr. Lane at once. To have another civilized being on the island! I was selfish. I thought of myself as well as Jill. And yes, I even foresaw the possibility of her falling in love with you. But only in time, only when she was a young woman and not a tomboy who looked like a sailor lad. It seemed to me a possible salvation for her; a boy like you from England. A boy who could one day take her back with him. Jill is a strange girl in many ways. To you she probably seems abrupt and cruel. But what is cruelty in her father is, I think, very different in her. She told me you had seen her spiders. I saw them once myself and have never been back to her tree-house. To you and me they seem horrible. But she loves them. What is more, she has never been bitten. And if she finds beauty in them where we like birds and flowers, is she cruel? Mistaken? Or simply different? The heartless things she said about your dolphin—forgive her for them, Charlie. She genuinely believed him to be a vicious animal. Curk had taught her so. Furthermore"—and here she hesitated—"if you find certain qualities of, shall I say, womanliness in me, you may discover a few of them also in Jill. Do you know that I found her last night with *Sonnets from the Portuguese?* She had slipped it out of my library and never expected me to visit her in her room. She quickly hid it under the pillow and doesn't yet know that I caught her memorizing the most beautiful sonnet of all.

"How do I love thee…"

"What else?" She paused and shuddered. "But what you tell me of Curk is monstrous…monstrous. He dares to call you married? And to speak of the Goat Without Horns?"

"What did he mean, Elizabeth."

"I don't know," she said flatly. "I have heard the phrase many times since I came here. It seems to be a sacrifice, a propitiation of the Shark God worshipped by the Caribs. And somehow you and Jill are to participate. Perhaps he wishes to make you fertile parents who will bear him many grandsons."

"Goats are used in sacrifices all over the world. A goat without horns could be—"

"A native child."

"Or Jill's first born, if it were a girl. But I'm not going to make love to her!"

"Of course you're not, my dear." She clasped him against her breast and rocked him like a child. She seemed to him then not an invalid but the elemental earth mother, all wise, all-encompassing, her intuition more powerful than man's intelligence. "But Curk's wrath will be beyond belief. He has rarely been crossed. I have sometimes deceived him in some small matter but never openly defied him. Once a young Carib quarreled with him over a girl. They fought with staves and Curk, as always, won. The loser was thrown into the sea. He was a strong swimmer, but whenever he neared the shore he was driven back by Carib children with stones until he tired and sank. The sharks devoured his body."

"Jill had promised not to tell Curk that I refused her. I am to leave the island on the next boat from Martinique."

"Then you may trust her to keep her word, even if she must lie to her father." She held him to her with the urgency of a mother losing her child and a mistress losing her lover. He had been an open and affectionate child, never ashamed to be embraced by his mother in public, never ashamed to embrace, and he did not lie passively in Elizabeth's arms but returned her embrace with equal ardor; half child, half lover. "Such a little time we have had to be friends, my dear. But of course you must go. It means your life."

"And you will come too, Elizabeth! I will be your Robert Browning and carry you to safety! And Jill," he added with considerably less fervor. "Together we may be able to steal a dugout and row out to the boat from Martinique."

"Do you really think that all three of us could leave this island without Curk's knowledge? Besides, Jill wouldn't want to go, and I—I lack the strength, my dear. I haven't the courage of our beloved Mrs. Browning. You must go alone with forgiveness in your heart for the sad, sick woman who brought you into such peril."

"For the great and gallant lady who has kept her courage and her beauty in spite of everything."

CHAPTER NINE

When Charlie came to me after his rejection of Jill and his meeting with Mrs. Meynell, he came to ask my help in escaping from Oleandra. He stripped down to his trousers; then shrugged and, even though on the side of the lagoon nearest to the Red House, removed them too, as well as his undergarments.

"To hell with the ladies. We've got a lot of traveling to do," he said. "I don't want to scratch you with bell-bottom trousers." He had still been wearing the rakish sailor garb which Jill had found for him on the one occasion when she had shown good taste. Nudity, however, was the proper state for swimming. Can you imagine a dolphin in pantaloons or even a loin cloth? Of course when he glided above me, holding my fin, his trousers did not hurt, but when he held me tightly for a dive or a leap, the coarse cloth of his britches, or even an undergarment with buttons, fretted my sensitive skin.

"Gloomer," he said, "I know there's a passage to the sea, or you couldn't have gotten in here in the first place. You've got to show it to me, though how I'm going to explain all this to you—"

I was already on my way to the passage. He had no time to ask me where I was heading—only to grasp my fin. He could hardly conceive that I had understood every word which he had just said to me. But I gave him no chance for questions. We reached an escarpment of sheer, plantless rock, and I shook free of him and dove a few feet under the surface to indicate the opening to the sea.

I returned to the surface and he supported himself with one hand on my flank and looked at me in a funny way.

"Gloomer, you understand a lot more English than I realized. You knew the word 'passage,' didn't you?"

As a matter of fact, I had already convinced him that I did understand a few English words. When he said "Dive," I dove; or "Come," I came; or "Stop," I stopped. But till now he had thought of himself like those dog fanciers who teach their pets some twenty or thirty commands and imagine that they have achieved a major breakthrough in communications, though I must repeat that he never patronized me, never tried to teach me tricks, never treated me as less than an equal. It was simply inconceivable to him that I should understand an English vocabulary almost as large as his, and it was my misfortune that my pronunciation was unintelligible to him. Even when I called him Charlie, he did not recognize his name, which to him resembled a human wheeze.

Now I answered him with a Delphinese "yes," actually a kind of prolonged clicking of the tongue, with no help from my airhole, hoping thereby to teach him a word but failing as usual. Then I made what I hoped was an approximation of the English "yes" which came out, even to my ears, between a squeak and a hiss—sort of an "iss." Finally I had to fall back on gestures. Dolphins, though markedly free with their bodies, have no movements to signify assent or dissent. We are far too literate. But for Charlie's sake I made the ridiculous motion of shaking my head up and down with a vehement splash.

"Yes!" he cried. "You're saying 'yes.' You understand practically everything I say, don't you?"

Another tremendous splash.

He gave me a hug. "Why you sly old fox." (Some English idioms still elude me; how I resembled a fox it was hard to comprehend, and how he could be calling me "sly" and "old" and complimenting me at the same time, as the hug indicated, defied explanation.) "I've told you everything about myself and you've taken it all in, haven't you? And I don't even know a thing about you except…except that you're the best friend I ever had!" It is quite extraordinary for an Englishman to be rhapsodic about friendship to your face. Generally, you have to surmise if he likes you by the warmth with which he calls you "old chap," or "sly old fox".

"You could know everything about me if you chose," I wanted to say. "And my race and all of what we know. How would you like to hear what Aristotle said to a dolphin in the year 333 B.C. ('You ought to be living on the land. Where am I going to put you in my encyclopedia?') Just let me teach you!" I was moved, honored, and frustrated at the same time and wanted desperately to tell him, but I reclined in the water and contented myself with looking pleased.

And then he told me the events of the day, which I have already told you, and how he had to leave the island in time to meet the boat from Martinique, which came the third day of each month, usually in the morning (depending on the winds). It was due in something less than three weeks. We would have to arrive early at the sea-entrance of the passage and wait in the water until it arrived and swim out to meet it before any Carib dugouts could precede or impede us.

It was not a foolproof plan. I was not as trusting as Charlie and Mrs. Meynell that Jill would remain tight-lipped about her rejection. I could see her running to daddy Curk and demanding immediate vengeance on the wretched boy who had dared to reject a Carib princess. And even if she chose not to betray Charlie, Curk had an uncanny way of appearing where he was unexpected, and knowing what was meant to be unknown to him. But it seemed the only possible plan. Had I been able to converse with Charlie, I might have suggested a devious safeguard. Why not satisfy the foolish girl, pretend that he meant to stay on the island with her, and thus avoid suspicion? After all, though boyish and bony, she was not exactly a hag, and Charlie needed experience in that direction. Mrs. Meynell, I felt, in spite of her beauty, was too old for him. But we dolphins look on sexual matters far more freely than do Englishmen. Perhaps it was just as well that I couldn't communicate that idea to him.

Once I saw him safely on board his boat, I would, of course, follow him to Martinique. And what then? He had talked alarmingly of a return to England. Perhaps a little time on the pleasant French island would convince him that not all of the West Indies were like Oleandra. Let him book passage on one of those island-plying vessels and I would follow in his wake and meet him on many-beached Tobago or fortressed Antigua and we would frolic through the pearly, perilous seas till I was an aged thirty like the Old Bull, and then he could build a hut above a quiet lagoon and we would commune when we could no longer frolic, and when I died he would deliver me to the islandless deep and to the watery Elysium of the Great Triton. In spite of Darwin, he worshipped his own God and believed in his own heaven, but perhaps in time he would come to prefer mine, since the Great Triton, also known as Davy Jones, is half man, and has welcomed many a sailor into his realm.

And if he did choose England? I refused to consider the prospect. There are dolphins who are born in those chilly northern waters and flourish in them. Perhaps I could learn. Certainly I could keep up with his ship, even one of those new iron steamships with paddle-wheels and screen propellers. But England's beaches are for holidays, not permanent living, and I could hardly expect Charlie to settle, say, at Brighton just to keep me company. He would probably return to Cambridge and finish his degree, and the fresh water Cam River was out of the question for my home. Lord Byron had kept a bear at Cambridge, but the bear had lived in his attic. I chose not to think about England.

We traversed the entire passage to the sea, I guiding him through a darkness only my eyes could pierce, around the occasional convolutions and across a tiny underground lake which shone like a fallen sky with starry noctilucas while Charlie cried out with the wonder of the place. At one point the passage was entirely filled with water, but he clutched me tightly (I being grateful for no bell-bottom trousers or buttons), held his breath, and trusted me to return him soon to the air. Once again there was space above our heads, and then the passage narrowed to the width of a single body, and he loosed my fin and followed me into the Caribbean, protected from its turbulence by a great rock jutting between us and the sea but feeling the current pull at his body. If this were the day for our escape, Charlie could cling on the leeward side of the rock, unseen by prowling Caribs, while I watched for the necessary schooner. But no, he had nearly three more weeks to spend with that girl and her gracious, beauteous, but pliant mother.

We did not linger in the sea because I wanted no snooping shark to catch our scent and follow us into the lagoon. Once we had returned to the lagoon, each of us a little scratched from the final ingress into the sea but buoyed with what seemed an excellent plan of escape, Charlie said:

"Gloomer, you're getting slimmer and faster every day. I'll bet you're the fastest dolphin in the West Indies!"

I made deprecating noises but I was immensely pleased. I was no longer a plump dolphin who ate to forget his grief. Not that I had forgotten my mother. I grieved for her every day. But my concern for Charlie was stronger than my grief. And there was something else. I felt that I had to be in the best possible shape for our escape. Suppose, in the next two weeks, I swam too near the shore or snoozed in the mangrove swamp and suddenly found myself with spears being hurled at me. Suppose the Caribs took after me in dugouts as I was carrying Charlie to the passage or from the passage to the boat from Martinique. A plump dolphin would be little use to himself or his friend. I was not yet quite an adult. I still had some growth ahead of me, but I was rapidly becoming among dolphins what Charlie was among boys: a redoubtable combination of youth, agility and energy. The Great Tark help any hammerhead I rammed in the belly.

"But Gloomer, you've scratched your beautiful skin!" Charlie cried.

I dove to the bottom of the lagoon and returned with a particularly insignificant piece of sea-weed between my jaws.

"Should I rub it on you?"

I presented my wounded flank. He crushed the plant in his hand and a white juice flowed out like milk from a cactus. Very gently his big hands massaged my wound and the smart rapidly disappeared.

But his own shoulder revealed a welt which he had overlooked. I snorted indignantly and pointed with my snout. (To what gesticulations our language barrier had reduced me!)

"Oh, that's nothing."

He was not even going to medicine himself. I caught his arm between my jaws and guided his still milky hand to his own wound.

He smiled. "I didn't know how much it was hurting until it stopped. Thank you, Gloomer. You're a physician as well as a friend."

"And a historian," I would have liked to add. I earnestly wanted him to know that I intended to compose his history as my life's chief work. It was the greatest compliment I could pay him.

When Charlie left me, I felt my usual wistfulness but also a momentary exhilaration. We were united by a great adventure and the very danger was provocative to a dolphin who had gloomed and moped for several months. I had little doubt that I could rescue Charlie from that dangerous island, and the comradeship of adventure promised to bind us as tightly as the halves of a closed clam.

But exhilaration soon yielded to anxiety. Hardly had Charlie climbed the hill to the Red House than I saw a black dorsal fin scything the surface, and almost at the same time I opened my mouth and tasted the rankness of shark in the water. I thought at first that the fellow had followed my scent through the passage. But there had been no sharks in the area when Charlie and I had emerged into the sea. Furthermore, this was a relatively small fellow, a five-foot, adolescent hammerhead, and I did not think he would deliberately have sought out a confrontation with a dolphin. Either he had blundered into the passage in spite of his poor eyesight, or he had been directed or summoned. Sharks are hopelessly stupid and unteachable. They operate purely on the level of instinct: swim, kill, eat, and rest. But instinct can be manipulated by a clever human as readily as intelligence. How else are ignorant pigeons made to carry messages? I surmised the manipulations of Curk.

At any rate, the lagoon was no longer a place for joyful frolicking. I charged directly at the interloper; maybe I could startle him back through the passage if he could remember its whereabouts. He skittered out of my path with much more fright than fight. I would have overtaken and engaged him if I had known for certain that he was a loner and not the first of a school. His eyes, widely spaced and protrusive, made him very vulnerable to my buttings. But I strongly suspected that he would soon be followed by larger friends. The Man Who Swam with the Sharks would hardly deign to swim with a single insignificant hammerhead. It behooved me to find a sanctuary, a place where no shark or sharks, however large, could threaten me, and no Caribs could threaten Charlie. In other words, a sea-cave which contained both earth and water and whose entrance could be concealed. I set out for the mangrove swamp. If no sanctuary existed, I would build one among those marvelously adaptable roots and that soft, sodden earth. Perhaps it was at that moment that I became an adult.

Generally a mangrove swamp is a paradise for adventurous dolphins. We can navigate among its canals much better than big, lumbering, dim-eyed sharks and visit with lackadaisical sea-cows, who never lose their tempers and who look as if they are listening to our histories even when they have fallen asleep. We can feast ourselves on delicacies not found in the open sea: tiny crabs and eels of swallowable dimensions; the egrets, the herons, the mangrove bushes themselves, with their cigar-shaped fruit, delight our sense of color, movement, and variety. However, we also know the perils, the moccasins, the strangling vines, the danger, of getting lost from the sea or grounded in a mud flat and baked by the sun when the tide recedes. And in this particular swamp, were the shiftless and bloodthirsty Caribs.

Fortunately, they were few in number—twenty adults and ten children—and they were not very venturesome. Because of their native indolence, which they cultivated as other men cultivate talents, they subsisted rather than lived. They had built their shacks on the solid ground near the main path and managed to deface only a small area by littering garbage in their front yards and penning goats and pigs in their back yards. Curk himself ruled them but disdained their company and, as I have said, lived in one of the English cottages near the Red House.

In my explorations, I came a little too close to a shack and a horrid child pelted me with rotten banana skins. He had been torturing his dog until I arrived; Carib dogs look like their masters, lean and shifty, but who can blame them, poor things, with such models? Garbage is their only diet, and even then they must scavenge in refuse heaps while children tweak their ears and parents kick them in the stomach. I caught a particularly decomposed banana skin between my jaws and returned it with force and frenzy, striking the child in the face. While he was blubbering his indignation, the tortured dog gave him a good nip on the leg and made his escape. So did I. Sanctuary did not lie in these parts.

I found what I was seeking nearer the lagoon. Guided by instinct more than eyesight, I thrust my nose through a tangle of greenery, which yielded to disclose a chamber so extraordinary that I thought: I have entered the palace of the Great Triton! This is his anteroom and soon his attendant mermen will appear to escort me to Elysium! I was vexed that I had been allowed to die before I had rescued Charlie. Then I realized with an immense relief that I was not, after all, in his palace, but rather in a place of his choosing and under his protection. The nacreous light reflected his sublimity and surely betokened the fact that here lay asylum for Charlie and me.

The roof was not of earth or vegetation, for I was not in a mangrove cave. With a twinkling of wonder I saw that it was mother-of-pearl. I was confronting a miracle shown to few dolphins and fewer men, a gigantic conch shell as big as a series of small caves. Such shells had thrived in the days when dolphins first took to the sea. Later the owners had become extinct, but here and there, beyond the waves and buried under the earth or hidden by vegetation, a shell remained, undimmed and undiminished, and I knew that I had found the best of sanctuaries. Envision a huge pink conch rather like the kind used by the natives as horns, but infinitely larger, with a pool and a dry ledge of shell just inside the long slit of the entrance; and with a series of connected water-filled chambers winding downwards and out of sight. I followed the narrowing chambers down to the last and smallest, which ended with the point of the shell, and then I ascended, whorl after whorl, darkness to dimness to light, into the highest chamber with its projecting shelf. Clearly, the Great Triton had directed me to asylum.

But we dolphins have a favorite epigram: "The Great Triton helps helpless little ones, but big ones must help themselves." Perhaps I was still young enough to deserve a measure of help, but only if I made the most of much. If a shark should follow my scent from the lagoon, there was nothing to keep him from charging through the thin screen of mangrove trees. The sublimity of the place would not deter him. Such creatures have no sense of propriety and no sense of deity. The formidable and finny god Tark is worshipped by the Caribs and not by the sharks themselves, who are much too stupid to think that the world did not create itself for the sole purpose of housing them in its waters and providing fish (and sailors) for their bellies.

With snout, flippers, and tail, I began to construct a barrier. I tangled the mangroves to such an extent that a shark would, I hoped, hesitate to entangle himself and, losing patience, prowl in other parts. In case he persisted and broke through the vines, I dredged up rocks from the bottom of the water outside the conch and pushed them into a crude barricade which retained a passage only large enough for Charlie or me. Once inside, we could finish our wall with a few more stones and also break our scent. You know how skilful we are with our snouts; or in crude human jargon, "bottle noses." We are always having to catch and carry to amuse human beings, and I was not the first of my race to put such a skill into building a wall. When I left my conch-shell house—and I left it provisioned with bananas (for Charlie) and fish (for me) in case of a siege—I observed with pride that no ordinary, weak-eyed, weak-brained shark could spot or suspect a cave behind the entanglement of mangroves and the rock wall. Then I returned to the lagoon to see if the hammerhead had been joined by friends. Otherwise, I felt that I could no longer tolerate his presence. I had not given chase or battle since the death of my mother. Since that time I had lost weight and gained strength. I wished both to test my new prowess and to secure the lagoon at least temporarily for Charlie, in case he should scramble in for a swim without spotting the invader.

But in the lagoon a disquieting sight awaited me: five hammerheads, including the original invader. I could hardly take on the lot of them. I had found my sanctuary none too soon. They flickered toward me, retreated, advanced, retreated, keeping always a space of water between us. As often as not a dozen sharks will encounter a lone dolphin and not attack him. Then one of them will suddenly change his mind and begin that great deadly sweep, and the others will forget their cowardice because of their superior numbers and attack, though at random and without any plan of battle such as killer whales devise. But not today. Assured that I was alone and no threat to them, they moved across the lagoon and began to feed in the fishy shallows.

 I was not so much frightened by their presence as infuriated. The lagoon had belonged to Charlie and me. Here we had become friends. Here I could look after him. Then I remembered what I should not have forgotten, that all of the island including the lagoon belonged to Curk, and now he was simply reclaiming what he had not needed for a while. I had no doubt that it was he who had summoned the sharks. Was it almost time for the Goat Without Horns? If so, the "goat" could hardly be Jill's first-born daughter. What else then? Though ignorant of Carib customs, I wracked my brain for a historical precedent in other lands. Some of the ancient Minoans, I recalled, though commendably kind to dolphins and fond of portraying us in their frescoes, had not always been so gracious to each other—indeed, to their own kings. Every year they had chosen a new king and every year, as soon as he had impregnated the queen, he had been sacrificed to secure the fertility of the fields.

CHAPTER TEN

Three weeks and four days: had he been so long on the island? The nights had passed in a mist of love; the days in lessons with Jill—polite, always polite now, but strained with awkward silences and reproachful eyes. Occasionally a visit to the lagoon (but no more swims—the sharks were idle but ever-threatening). Soon, the boat from Martinique. Soon, his flight from Oleandra, from danger and, alas, from love.

Dinner that night was one whose silences were broken only by the gracious but half-hearted sallies of Elizabeth. Guilt was a fourth guest in the room. Charlie was unashamed of his love for Elizabeth, indeed, proud; but Jill reminded him, with every gesture and every silence, that he had rejected her in favor of her mother, wounded her pride and broken her heart. Had she told her father? Did she mean to tell him? It was she who had summoned guilt to the banquet; guilt and apprehension.

Charlie marveled at Elizabeth's composure. She surmounted not only the awkwardness of the occasion, but the folds and intricacies of a dress whose magnificence was matched by its magnitude. Its green-silver silk, trimmed with red roses to the tip of the train, rippled and coruscated in the light of the candelabrum. The sweet and artful dishevelment of her hair, the golden ringlets escaping down her back; he thought of Rapunzel in the old fairy tale, she whose hair had become a ladder for a knight to climb in order to rescue her from the witch who kept her imprisoned. No longer did he think of her as an older woman, beautiful but august, who had engaged him to tutor her daughter. She was his own beloved Elizabeth, to whom he was drawn with an idealistic yearning which did not need to deny her faults, and also with the sheer physical hunger of an inexperienced but ardent boy for a beautiful and deliberately seductive woman.

Even Jill had worn a dress to dinner: a cream silk patterned with daffodils. She had also combed her hair and, short though it was, she looked distinctly feminine though ill at ease. She was trying to rearrange the long skirt and accommodate herself and her dress to the chair. As for Charlie, he was none too comfortable himself in his long frock coat of broadcloth with velvet-laced lapels, together with waistcoat and gold Prince Albert watch chain. Except for Elizabeth's sallies, the three of them were locked into a tableau of formal clothes and stiff manners. He felt that if they spoke at all, they should speak epigrams out of Congreve or Sheridan. It was then that the drum began in the Carib village. The candelabrum, with its host of roseate angels, swayed above their heads; the goblets tinkled on the table. The drum did not play to summon or lament, but rather to exult; storms reverberated in its exultance, and the wind which compelled the waves, and a torrid tropic sun, and animals too: birds and fish, eagles and barracudas, the swiftest, the strongest, all things wild, unfettered, elemental, uniting in a fierce paean of joy.

"It's nothing to be frightened of," said Jill tartly, though no one had expressed any fright. "It's just a simple drum four feet high and made of bamboo, with a black goatskin pegged across the top."

"Nobody's frightened," said Charlie. "Just mystified. Is it Curk playing?"

"Who else?"

"Is it for a festival of some kind?"

"It could just as easily be for a funeral. The drum plays on both occasions."

He was sick of evasions and reticences. "The funeral of The Goat Without Horns?"

She stared at him as if she expected Tark to punish his blasphemy with a waterspout hurled from the depths. "I don't know what you mean."

"What I mean is this. First, the sharks. Now the drum. Jill, what in the name of Tark is going to happen?"

"The boat from Martinique is due in three days, as you doubtless know. I expect you'll go aboard her and leave our little island to its mysteries."

"Well, at any rate we've had enough mystery for one night," Elizabeth interjected, reasserting her supremacy over the gathering. "Let's imagine that we're dining with William Morris who felt that beauty and simplicity were the same thing." Plainly she feared the frankness of Charlie's questions or Jill's answers. Elizabeth embraced the room with an expressive sweep of her hand, and Charlie contemplated the plain, scrubbed, but ruggedly beautiful oak of the table, the willow-patterned china, the small chairs with plaited osier seats, the red Gothic sideboard, the tapestry of gold thread on woolen twill, illustrating Chaucer's illustrious women. And most of all, the room itself with its high-ceiling and exposed beams.

But his thoughts were not with Morris.

"And you even have a fireplace," he forced himself to remark. "Morris still loves an open fire, they say. It sets him off on one of his stories. And he will never let anyone paint the natural bricks or clutter the mantle in any of his houses." He was trying to think of Morris; he was trying not to think about the black land crabs steamed in greens which lay untouched on his plate and which were, according to the dictates of his stomach, untouchable. He was mostly thinking about Elizabeth and wondering, what with sharks and drums and Goats Without Horns, if he could prevail upon her to leave the island with him.

"Yes, I had to have a fireplace, though it's rather absurd in this warm climate. Still, the nights do get chilly at times, and then I light my fire. It makes me feel as if I were back in England again."

"And I noticed something else," said Charlie. "All the food stays hot until it reaches the table. You took Morris' advice about where to build the kitchen."

"Build it close to the dining room!" (Most English houses separated the kitchen from the dining room with a host of lesser chambers, and the last guests to be served usually received cold squabs in coagulated gravy or blackberries swimming in melted ices.)

Suddenly Jill flung back her chair and sprang to her feet, overlooking Telesphorus who, muffled in his hood and muffled of step, had crept behind her to refill her goblet with port. The copper flagon fell from his hand and bounced soundlessly but wetly over the rug, dispersing drops like a garden sprinkler. While Telesphorus' father bustled in apologetically from the kitchen to dry up the spilled wine, Jill glared at Charlie and then at her mother, as if to lock them into a single conspiracy.

"You and your poets. How can you talk about William Morris tonight?" Where was the Jill to whom he had given the fiddler crab; the wistful girl who had accepted his rejection with grave resignation?

He was losing patience. "Jill, do you know what is going to happen tonight? If you do, I wish you would enlighten us."

"No." The answer was sullen as well as ambiguous. He had supposed her to be in her father's confidence, but her explosion and evasiveness suggested uncertainty or perhaps a knowledge too terrible either to contain or share.

"The Caribs haven't had a festival for years," said Elizabeth, "and unfortunately they don't have many funerals. Unless they happen to knife each other in a moment of pique, they just make love or lie in the sun like alligators and live to a lecherous old age."

"You have no right to talk about them like that," Jill shouted. "They're a poor little remnant of a great people, and you ought to dwell on their past instead of criticizing them now." She flounced out of the room, rushing, no doubt, to muss her hair and don her sailor togs.

Telesphorus had vanished into the kitchen with his father, who was muttering parental rebukes while his son was pleading, "But I didn't dent the flagon." Charlie and Elizabeth looked at each other with a shared helplessness which made Charlie, at least, feel much less helpless. He took her hand across the table.

"Has she told him I rejected her?" Charlie asked.

"I don't think so."

"Does he know about us?"

"No. His pride will admit no rivals. His pride, I say, not his heart. You see," she added, a little wistfully, "it isn't love he feels for me. It's possession. I am no longer a necessity or a novelty to him, only a habit. All I can say for myself is that I am a difficult habit for him to break."

She put a cautioning finger to her lips as Telesphorus returned to serve the desert of papaya balls soaked in rum and lime juice. The little orange globes swam in transparent amethyst goblets, like suns in a galaxy.

Charlie recaptured her hand as soon as the boy had returned to the kitchen. "Elizabeth, I'm not sorry. I shall never be sorry, unless Curk harms you. But that's not going to happen. You're coming to England with me." At this point handholding seemed to him singularly inadequate. He raised her hand to his lips and kissed her fingertips and deliberated if he could attain the mouth before the next entrance of the domestics.

"It's you, my dear, who may be hurt."

"I don't think so," he said stoutly, if not with complete conviction. "What is Curk's strength, really? Mystery, more than anything else, wouldn't you say? Nobody knows him, not even you, after sixteen years. But if we could see through him, mightn't we find just a big bully who rules over a scraggly bunch of savages?"

"No, Charlie. Whatever he is, he's not like us. His mystery, I'm afraid, is as terrible as we imagine. If you ever doubt that, look in the lagoon where you swim with your friend. Or used to. This morning from my bedroom I saw a sight to freeze my blood. Jill was clambering over some tumbled rocks, black and lava-like, which spilled right down into the water. She scurried over them with the agility of her tarantulas, carrying a basket under her arm. There was a final rock which jutted over the water like a small ledge. She knelt, drew off the cover from the basket, and removed a fish. Three black fins converged on the bait.

"Jill," I cried, but she could not, or would not, hear me from such a distance.

"As gently as a dog from his master's hand, the first of the hammerheads took the fish. His companions did not disturb his feast. Restraint among sharks. Unthinkable! Then I saw that Jill was not alone. A solitary figure loomed on the cliff above her head. She had known that he was close to her. She looked up at him and he smiled and nodded his approval."

"You think he's trained them not to harm her?"

"At least when he's close to her. I think he has actually taken her swimming with them in the sea. If she swam alone, who can say? They're almost totally instinctive, and Curk is the only man I ever knew who could control that instinct."

Charlie shuddered. "And Jill thinks they're beautiful. She trusts them as she does her spiders."

"You're very fond of her, aren't you?"

"In a way, I am. Fond of and sorry for."

"Find her, will you Charlie? She won't have gone far at night. Not even Jill ventures beyond the village after dark."

"What shall I say to her?"

"That we miss her in the house. Try to convince her not to tell her father that she is, how shall I say, not with child by you."

She was sitting under the acacia trees and looking as if she would like to cry but did not intend to let Charlie or anyone else see her a second time in so undignified and undisguised a state. She had not mussed her dress or her hair, and she might have been an English school girl who had been neglected at her first ball. She spoke in a whisper, but the drum had stopped and he could understand her in the deep stillness of the night, whose only voice was the small, sweet piping of an occasional tree-frog.

She met him with an accusation. "You've come to ask me if I told my father about your scorning me."

"No."

"But Mother asked you to ask me, didn't she?"

"I came because I wanted to."

"You think I'm still angry because you preferred mother. You see, I know you spent the night with her. Two nights, in fact. At first I was furious with both of you. I almost went to Curk. I wanted him to hurt you, and Mother too. But then I realized why it was you couldn't love me. Because you had loved Mother first. Since that very first night, I think. It was wrong of you to love her, but she is very beautiful and you were lonely. And I took you to her myself, didn't I? In a sense, you were being faithful to your first love. A woman likes a man to be faithful. Even to her rival, at first. Then, when she finally wins him, her triumph is doubled. Otherwise, she will value him lightly as too easily won. I only wish I had been first."

He noticed a subtle but significant change in her use of the word "love" which he could not ascribe to her reading. She no longer sounded as if she were speaking about copulation among the Caribs.

"I do love her," he said. "She's like a Christmas evergreen hung with garlands and berry-chains. Even when she's still she somehow twinkles and dazzles."

"And I do forgive you. I guess I'm more of a young fir tree. Hard and prickly."

"A sapling, I should say, and strong rather than prickly. But have you also forgiven your mother for—being fond of me?"

She shrugged helplessly. "I stay angry with her about half the time. I used to think it was because she was so different from me, soft and pampered and frilly, with a wastefully large bosom. But since you came, I think it's because I'm so different from *her*. Yes, I've forgiven her for loving you. But not for being beautiful and golden and loved by you."

"But you have your own kind of beauty. Your mother is a bird of paradise. You're a—" The poet in him strained for a metaphor which would please her, "a quicksilver tarpon. Quicker than a dolphin!" (Indeed!)

He patted her shoulder, a brother with a younger sister, and said nothing, because there was nothing more of comfort which he could say. His gesture was protective and instinctive and totally lacking in amorous intent.

She lifted the arm from her shoulder. "You're just making it worse. If we're going to be buddies, I think we should restrict ourselves to a manly handshake."

"But that was a manly pat," he tried to explain. "The kind I give Gloomer."

"But it means something different to me. You feel as if you're just patting me hello or maybe keeping me warm. But I tremble all over like…" He awaited one of her stark metaphors. "…a shower-of-gold petal caught in a breeze."

"No embraces then. Just handshakes."

"Well, maybe now and then a little one." She replaced his arm and did not set limits on the duration of its visit. "Now I've kept two secrets for you," she said at last. "Your rejecting me and your fondness for my mother. That makes us very special friends, doesn't it?"

"It certainly does."

"As close as you and that dolphin?" Having discussed his love for her mother with surprising candor, she was a little girl again, pleading for affection.

Charlie could not lie even to be tactful (if I were one of the old, land-dwelling dolphins with limbs, I would have hugged him for his honesty).

"Gloomer is my best friend. Remember, I met him before I met you. But you're special to me too."

She looked pensive. "I suppose I'll have to be content, though it would be so much nicer to be very special. It isn't flattering when you lose out to a dolphin, though maybe this one can be trusted after all. At least, he hasn't tried to eat you, and he's had a great many chances. The way you undress, he wouldn't have even had to worry about indigestion from cloth or buttons. I did notice a scar on your shoulder, though. Did he nip you there?"

"I bruised myself on a rock, and Gloomer healed me with some juice from seaweed." He trusted her—for the moment—but he was not going to tell her about the passage to the sea. Girls of fifteen had been known to change their minds; Jill changed her mind as often as the sea changed its moods. The simile seemed to him unoriginal but nonetheless applicable.

"If he only weren't so ugly." She deliberated. "And yet you like your women all golden and fluffy. I would expect you to make friends with a parrot fish instead of a dolphin. Or perhaps—"

"My children, it is time."

They had not been aware of Curk's approach until he knelt behind them and enfolded them in a single embrace. They both started to their feet. He smiled. It was a night of smiles, encouraging, conspiratorial, wistful, and now triumphant.

"For The Goat Without Horns?" Jill's voice faltered with rare fear. Was it possible that she did not know the nature of the ritual?

"Yes."

"Where, my Father?"

"On the Cliff that Looms Like a Shark." His words were forbidding but his voice held the tenderness of a devoted parent. His arm around Charlie's shoulder was almost paternal. It was also irresistible. It held and compelled him toward the place for which, knowingly or not, he had been bound since he had read the advertisement in the *London Times*.

Childe Roland to the Dark Tower Came.

CHAPTER ELEVEN

Wordlessly they exchanged their clothes for the garments offered to them by the wordless Curk; the garments of the festival. With the joyous abandonment of a moth which sheds its chrysalis, Jill shed her ankle-length frock, her Englishness and her innocence, for a tight leather tunic with beads woven into intricate designs of sea anemones and coral forests. With abandonment which was anything but joyous, Charlie exchanged his frock coat for a loin cloth like that of Curk.

"I'm a bloody savage," he thought.

Curk surveyed them with familial pride. He seemed to make no distinction between them now that he thought them mates.

"It is time, my children. You are ready—and worthy."

No one spoke as they climbed the side of the cliff, but Charlie's mind was a colosseum of conflicting selves. The gladiator in him said: act now, break loose from this magnificent but slit-cheeked savage before he delivers you to his friends; attack him or flee from him. The martyr said: if he meant to harm you, would he treat you like a son? Besides, there is no escape from him on this island. At least go with him to the cliff and learn his intention.

The path was precipitous and seemed to have been oftener climbed by goats than men. There were treacherous stones which slipped from under foot and sheer vertical rises with only roots for hand- or foot-holds. But there were resting places of verdurous moss overhung with frangipani trees, and the air was sweet with the fragrance so beloved by Elizabeth. Yet it seemed the wrong scent for such a night and place. There should be what? Incense, perhaps, frankincense or myrrh. Something a little acrid and—sacrificial.

Charlie had often been mountain-climbing in Scotland, and there were no difficulties for him on this small cliff, except that of keeping up with Jill, who had played her solitary games in just such places, if not in this very place. Curk did not seem to climb or scramble so much as to ascend. There was no effort in his movements, no labored breaths or pauses to rest; there was assurance and ease and most of all dignity. Instead of a slit-cheeked savage, he seemed the genius of the mountain vouchsafing guidance to those who aspired to his heights.

The top of the cliff was hidden for most of the climb. Then, suddenly, they stood among pine-knot torches, a forest of writhing brilliances. The darkness had been protective; the light was a nakedness and a confrontation.

The altar was one of the high places of the Old Testament, but pagan, Philistine, not Israelite; not dedicated to Yahweh, for its stones were shaped into the semblance of a deity with the head and shoulders of a shark and the body of a man, a reversal of the fish-tailed Dagon whose temple Samson had leveled. The Caribs, the twenty adults from the village, had assembled beside the altar. Noisy chatterers by day, indolent and decadent, they stood now with the stillness of stones as their, king, his daughter, and his—disciple? captive?—approached them. In the torchlight it was possible to imagine them as their own ancestors at the height of their power before the coming of the Spaniards—barbaric with black slit cheeks and golden earrings in the form of sharks, and yet with a ghost of sublimity imparted by their adoration of Curk. He was their master; he was their god as well as Tark; only he could remember the old way and conjure them momentarily out of their indolence and decadence.

The Caribs moved from the altar and out of the torchlit circle and hovered like vertical shadows beyond the light. Curk moved into the circle with Jill and Charlie. He lifted his arms to pray in a gesture immemorially older than the familiar kneeling of Christians, yet in his words rang cadences learned from the Bible.

We have fallen from the mountaintops. Travailed in the valleys of shadow while inferior beings frolicked among our cloudlands. Combatted demons and felt the scream of their shafts. But the time has come for the fallen to arise; the conquerors to fall. Our god has not forsaken us, nor has he suffered wounds from the spears of the conquerors. He has walked with us in our exile, quietly, quietly, until we could not hear his tread. But quietness is not his accustomed way. Through me he thunders; through me he speaks to you.
'Curk,' he has said. 'Give me a gift to delight my heart, and I will uplift your people to their old eminence.'
'Father,' I replied. 'What gift shall my people and I, thus fallen, find to pleasure you?'
'I am lonely,' he said. 'In the sea I find no companion except my sharks; on the mountaintops, I walk without comrades though the goats roam in herds and the hawk has her nest of young. I, though a god, may suffer a human travail. Find me a daughter and son to bear a child in my name. Consecrate him to me, who shall be his father and brother, teacher and friend. Then you shall climb the mountain of your lost mornings.'
'Father,' I said. 'I will do this thing. I will bring you my own flesh, my own beloved daughter, whom I have reared to your glory. I will bring you the stalwart youth whose strength has quickened her loins. I will yield you these, my children, to be your children, and they in turn will yield you their unborn child.'

An Ancient of Days he stood, though his face showed little age; a vessel of his god's command. His voice held the roll of thunder, his arm might have hurled a thunderbolt. And yet he wept. He who had swum with the sharks wept mortal tears.
He lowered his arms and the god was gone from him.

He held out his hands and drew Jill and Charlie into a single embrace. Slowly, with tenderness, he kissed Jill on the mouth.

"My daughter. You are without fear?"

"I am without fear, my father."

"My son, you shall fear for a little and then be fearless forever."

They had come to the edge of the cliff, the lights behind them, the sea before them, an opaque mirror of reflected torches and vast shadows; windless, motionless, flawless. The breaking of the mirror was without sound, but it seemed to resound in Charlie's ears. The reflected lights rippled, the shadows shifted, nothing more, but Charlie felt a horror of total loss, a desecration of Curk's prayer and the solemnity of the night. For the breakers were hammerheads.

The Caribs stiff with reverence; the prayer like a psalm; the motionless lagoon—these had been design and order; these had been beautiful. But chaos had come with the sharks, and to Charlie the ultimate horror was the fact that to everyone else they completed rather than broke the ritual, finished the magic circle to conjure Deity.

At the silent prompting of Curk, his hand outstretched to command and conjure, the Caribs joined him at the edge of the cliff. Exalted and exultant, they saw their god epitomized in the creature most dear to him. Both sharks and men, it seemed, had gathered for mutual homage to the god who swam in the sea like a shark or climbed the cliffs like a man.

Even Jill seemed to find a rightness in the coming of the sharks. She watched them without fear; tall and proud, a chieftain's child, ready to sacrifice herself like Jepthah's daughter.

The devil take such a ritual! thought Charlie. The devil is *in* the ritual. He had climbed the cliff and he meant to return the way he had come—with Jill. He touched her arm, not to steady her, for she did not need to be steadied—her grace was flawless—but to beseech her back to his world. But she was beyond his supplication.

Then, she was beyond his touch. Quicksilvering the night, she dove from the cliff. The Goat Without Horns...

At last he could act. At last he knew how to act. He did not stop to rationalize: she has fed the sharks from her own hands. Perhaps they will not harm her even when she dives among them. He saw a friend, more beloved than he had realized, in what seemed to him deadly peril. He had no choice. He would dive after her.

But even as he leaned from the cliff, he felt the implacable hands of Curk around his waist.

"Look, my son."

She was swimming with the sharks. She swam beside them, between them, among them, rested her hand on a cruel, misshapen head. She rippled the torchlight reflections, catching the light in her hair, herself like a newly lit torch. Light among darkness, she swam in that black-magicked sea and received no hurt.

They rose and sank around her, took her caresses, taking, always taking; giving neither love nor affection but taking the sensuous warmth from her hand, the hypnotic rhythm from her body.

She was laughing now; she dove, frolicked, flaunted her new-found powers. The motion of the sharks increased. They splashed beside her, nuzzled her, prodded her. The water began to foam and churn.

"I'm going to ride them!" she cried. "Like Charlie with his dolphin. Which one shall I ride?"

"Daughter!"

The word was command and caution. He had briefly loaned her his power; her immunity was not yet perfect.

"Yes, my father?"

"Enough. You have swum with the sharks and will again. Swim now to the beach. At once, my child, but without haste."

She obeyed with reluctant strokes, looking over her shoulder at her new friends and coaxing them to escort her on her journey.

Charlie watched her until she had climbed onto the beach, and Curk watched her until she had sought the path to the cliff and was hidden from both the lagoon and the place of the altar. Until it appeared that she could not see him.

"And now, my son. You too…"

Needless to say I had swum as close to the sharks and the cliff as I had dared. I was well aware that they could scent me, just as I could have scented any one of them, and together their rank, indescribable smell of blood and rotten melons assaulted my nostrils and almost turned my four stomachs. But they were not at the moment concerned with a lone dolphin. They were hearkening first to the man on the cliff, then to Jill.

I must admit that I watched her with real trepidation. For the first time, I felt a grudging fondness for her and a fear for her safety. Nobody, not even Curk's daughter, not even Curk, should trust a shark. But at least she had pleased herself and her father and, I hoped, completed the ritual for that dreaded night.

Dreadful night, I should say. It was then that I saw Charlie's fall or, because of my limited vision, that final part of the fall which he somehow turned into a partial dive.

I knew who had thrown him. I hated the thrower with a hatred which was sheer malevolence and which totally belied the popular notion of dolphins as playful and benign. I hated the thrower as I had hated the shark which had killed my mother. But anger was a wicked luxury unless I put it to work. For Charlie.

Evidently he had been flung, outward and downward, with such force that he would land with a stupefying splash and would excite the sharks to immediate attack. But he was as agile in the air as on the land and he managed to strike the lagoon with arms in front of him and to break the water without a frenzy of splashing. Quickly but quietly he rose to the surface among the slow-moving fins and slowly began to swim for the beach. When the sharks converged behind him, a ridiculous image flashed into my brain: six black pirate sails behind a Spanish treasure ship. Left to themselves, they might have followed him to shore and let him escape out of sheer lethargy or curiosity. Sharks have no sense of beauty but they do have a sense of rhythm, and the gliding body of Charlie lulled them and soothed them. Hypnotically he swam; hypnotized they followed but did not attack him.

It was then that I felt the compulsion hurled from the duff, a sheer animal energy which spoke to the sharks on the one level they could understand, that of pure instinct: KILL. For me, it was like being enveloped in the inky cloud of a squid; noxious, suffocating to the mind if not to the lungs.

I put my anger to use. I streaked toward Charlie at thirty knots and reached him ahead of the sharks.

He grasped my fin, he gasped my name, and we set out for my sanctuary like a Triton from the jaws of a whale. I could have attained the beach without difficulty, but once Charlie climbed ashore, the Caribs would doubtless come screaming down from the cliff, and he would have been rescued only to be recaptured while I was trapped by the sharks. Thus, I chose the swamp.

With the additional weight of Charlie, I could not hope to outswim the sharks in a long chase. But they floundered for several seconds before they began their pursuit. They were frightened; the smell of dolphin always disturbs them, and for all they knew I might be one of a herd. They were also bewildered. Curk's command was penetrating their tiny brains, but where was the man to be killed? Once their nostrils had told them that there was only one dolphin, who had joined his scent to that of the man, I had skirted around them and aimed for the mangrove swamp.

By the time I reached the swamp, they were close behind me; their smell was more than offensive, it was horrendous, and I could hear the ominously gentle rippling of water parted by fins.

But the swamp befuddled them. It was not their habitat; its meandering canals baffled their poor vision. They collided with sudden banks; they tangled themselves in the snaky mangrove roots; they became separated and frightened; and I, after circling, criss-crossing, and losing, I trusted, the last of them, made for the sanctuary.

I nuzzled my way through the concealment of vegetation and revealed the opening in my stone barricade. Then I withdrew and helped, or rather shoved, Charlie through the opening and followed him, restoring the vegetation behind me with my tail and, once I saw him safely on the ledge, lifting the stones in place with my beak to shut the entrance. Charlie handed them to me one at a time from the ledge.

"If you aren't the cleverest fellow," he said, patting my head when the last stone was in place. "You've saved my life, you know. I thought there was only one Goat Without Horns—or one and a half, counting Jill's hypothetical baby—but there seem to have been two, and I was the edible one."

Well, yes, he was the edible one and I had saved his life. But how could a friend do otherwise? I told him so in my best English.

"I keep thinking you're trying to tell me things," he said. "But I just can't understand what you're saying. Forgive me, old chap. And now I think we deserve a rest, don't you?" As for me, I felt no fatigue, but a marvelous exhilaration at having rescued my friend and brought him to my house. As for Charlie, he discovered my provisions and decided that he would rather eat than rest. The fish were some I had caught in the lagoon and beheaded with a neat chomp of my jaws. The bananas I had stolen from the Caribs, who had left a succulent bunch too close to a canal and within reach of my versatile snout. English schoolboys, like dolphins, can always eat, even when they have almost been eaten. "I guess we must just stay here for three days and then try to slip through to the passage and meet the boat."

Yes, that was the sensible thing to do. I acquiesced with my usual ungainly nod and pointed to another fish, meaning to suggest that he try it with his seventh banana. He misunderstood—purposely, I fear, since the fish was raw—and passed it to me, along with a banana, which he thoughtfully removed from its skin. The fish was a tasty mullet which I devoured with much relish, though I wanted to lecture him on the nutritional advantages of raw fish and the need for a balanced diet.

"And once on board, I shall lead a party ashore and rescue Elizabeth!" By now he was thoroughly enjoying our adventure. "And take Jill with us by force, if we have to."

I snorted; I have never been one to hide my emotions.

He came to her defense. "I don't think she had the least notion what was going to happen. Not to me anyway. Only to herself. Why else did Curk wait until she couldn't see him when he threw me to the sharks? He knew how horrified she would be. By now he's no doubt told her that I fell or jumped in to save her and got myself eaten."

I looked at him thoughtfully and concluded that for once his trust might be justified. No one who looked and talked like Charlie could fail to turn a young girl's heart. No, Jill could not have known what her father intended for him. Charlie was a hero unaware of his heroism. Stripped of his English tweeds and his sailor's garb, dressed in a loin cloth, he had ceased to be English; he had become Rousseau's Noble Savage (you see, I know my human philosophy as well as my human history).

While I was admiring Charlie and Charlie was vindicating Jill, we finished my entire stock of provisions down to one last overripe banana and a small, gristly looking fish.

"Gloomer, we have gorged ourselves," announced Charlie. "Tomorrow we shall have to go foraging among the mangroves. You don't think the sharks will—?"

The attack was more than sudden, it was instantaneous. My barricade did not so much yield as dissolve. We had been invaded; we were on the verge of being devoured; and the invader and devourer was a huge hammerhead, the ugliest if not quite the cruelest of all the sharks. Nature is sometimes deceptive; she has concealed poison in the beautiful, tapering leaves of the oleander, but in the hammerhead, she wrought to reveal the soul. With his cruel flat head like a mallet and his wide-spaced, ogling eyes, he is what he seems: both scavenger and killer.

My first thought was: Charlie, press yourself against the wall. He can't get to you on the back of the ledge. My second thought was to join Charlie. Many a dolphin while chasing an elusive fish has dived into a boat or onto a beach. I could breathe on the ledge and remain fairly comfortable until my skin began to dry. My third thought, which coincided with rather than succeeded the second, was that the Great Triton had created sharks in error, or perhaps inherited them from an older Creation, and dolphins were meant to rectify the error or the inheritance. This one looked huge and arrogant, but size might work against him in so small a space. Had not the lumbering galleons of the Spanish Armada reeled before the swift small pinnaces of England?

The shark was surrounded by the debris of the barricade—leaves, bits of mangrove branches, stones—and was still a little confused by his new and constricted surroundings. He had doubtless scented me by now, probably seen me, but not yet attacked me. He was four times my length; his skin was hard and murderously abrasive. The teeth in his flattened head were a multiple horror. I chose to go for his eyes, which were peculiarly vulnerable because they protruded from his head. If I could blind him, he could still scent me. But the pain might drive him from the shell and the loss of one sense would at least limit his maneuverability. I rammed him in the left eye and he recoiled with a suddenness which sent a small wave rolling over the ledge. Charlie, by the way, was leaning over the ledge with a sharp stone which he had rescued from the debris, awaiting his chance.

Now for the other eye. But he was growing warier and more at ease in the narrow confines of our battleground. He made a slow, calculated circuit of the chamber to gauge its shape and size and all the while he thrashed his head and tail to discourage attack. Now, now, I thought, and lunged at his other eye. But I badly misjudged his speed and took a terrific blow from his tail. I found myself bruised and breathless across the chamber from him. If he had caught me then he could have finished with his teeth what his tail had begun. I was not wounded but I was certainly winded.

A blur of images, again the horrible thrashing, Charlie on the ledge with empty hands, a stone which had somehow struck its mark and lodged in the shark's one good eye. (Charlie, Charlie, stay on the ledge! You've done all you can to help me.)

Charlie was out of stones. He was climbing into the water to replenish his supply and possibly, no, probably, lure the attacker until I had recovered my wind. (Idiot, stay where you are!)

I was forced into a dangerous expedient to regain the shark's attention. I flicked him insolently with my tail and dove into the second and smaller chamber. He could block my passage back to the air. Remember, I breathe through lungs, instead of gills. He could also attack Charlie. But I counted on his anger to spur him after me, and on his ignorance of how the chambers diminished in size.

There was scarcely room for him in the second chamber. His body full-length stretched from wall to wall. I dipped and rolled and somehow eluded both his teeth and the bruising walls, and dove as if I were entering the third and lowest chamber. Again he followed me. The smell of shark was rank in my lungs; he was like a plague of darkness descending on a happy land. At the last possible second, I somersaulted up from the entrance and over him and watched his enormous momentum carry him into the lowest, smallest chamber of the shell. He could not turn; he could only try to back; and I dove at his tail and caught it between my teeth. He thrashed like a boar in a net, strained away from me, and crammed his wide head into the lowest reach of the shell. His wounded eyes received an additional wounding; and whenever he tried to back, I assaulted his tail with my own by-no-means-negligible teeth and shredded the leathery skin.

In the end, he destroyed himself. It was not my attacks nor Charlie's stones. It was his own rage. He literally beat himself to death against the hard, unyielding shell, or so I judged from his convulsive agonies. The Great Triton had led me to the one battleground in which I could triumph over such an awesome adversary.

I did not remain to watch his final convulsions. I instinctively hated all sharks, and this shark had threatened my friend, but hatred ceases when the hated one dies without dignity in pain and humiliation.

I broke the surface in the highest chamber, my airhole working furiously, my body aching as if I had just been spewed from Edgar Allan Poe's maelstrom. I must have looked as if I had lost the fight.

"Gloomer, are you all right, old man?" He spoke from the ledge, amidst a pile of dripping stones.

"Iss."

"Iss. Yes? Yes! You're speaking English!"

"Isssss."

"You have been all along, haven't you, and I haven't been understanding. My God, old man, tell me what happened below!"

"Ease daid."

"Dead, you say? You've killed him, Gloomer? You've saved my life again!" He surveyed my bruises. "We must get you some healing seaweed. That is, as soon as we can get out of here. And how we shall talk, once I catch onto your English a little better!"

But there were other sharks in the lagoon, and Curk and the Caribs were waiting for Charlie, and I was tired and—

Below us we heard a muffled rumbling, scraping, creaking, as when a sunken vessel, shaken by an earthquake, lumbers toward the surface. The water reddened with blood. Charlie looked at me with consternation.

"You did kill him, didn't you?"

I remembered an adage taught to me by the Old Bull. "Confidence kills sharks; over-confidence kills dolphins."

Charlie grasped a stone; I waited with sick expectancy, no longer, I feared, a hero to my hero; tired to the bone, exhausted of strategems; ready to fight but expecting to lose.

"Never mind, we'll get him this time. But Gloomer. It… isn't…the…hammerhead."

It was the mutilated body of Curk.

CHAPTER TWELVE

Charlie and Jill had met in the dining room for their last dinner in the Red House. Tomorrow the schooner would come from Martinique; tomorrow they would depart for England. Was it only a night ago that they had dined, he with apprehension, she with a restless anticipation, to the beat of a Carib drum? To Charlie, tonight should have been a time to rejoice; Curk was dead; the sharks had left the lagoon. The Caribs, bereft of their leader, had departed from the island in their dugout canoes on another lap of their journey to oblivion. But what to him had been a victory had been to Jill a tragedy. She had lost her father; she had lost her adopted people, loved in spite of their degeneracy; and Charlie could not rejoice. He could only try to console.

She sat with moist eyes, gallantly withholding her tears, and she might have been one of those English girls, brave and silent, who sent their sweethearts, brothers, and fathers to die in England's interminable wars. He was glad that she did not know the full and ghastly circumstances of her father's death. She only knew that Charlie had come to the Red House in the dead of night, looking like a drowned sailor, and found her with Elizabeth as they sobbed in each other's arms, for him, not Curk, because they thought that he had drowned in the lagoon.

"Elizabeth, Jill," he had gasped. "Curk is dead." He was too weary to delay his shattering news, but at least he could soften it with evasions and omissions. "Gloomer took me to a half-submerged cave in the mangrove swamp, but Curk came after me. We fought on a ledge and he fell into the water. Gloomer killed him to save my life."

Jill had shrieked and run from the room.

"Dear God, we must hide you," Elizabeth had cried. "The Caribs will want your scalp."

"Not any more. They intercepted me on my way here from the swamp. I told them what had happened—there was nothing else I could do—and took them to Curk's body. I thought they would kill me on the spot, but they seemed to lose all spirit. They didn't throw spears at Gloomer and they didn't try to stop me from coming to you. They almost seemed afraid of us. I think they felt as if their god had let them down, and they were disgraced because of him. Disgraced and frightened."

But that was last night. He had waited for Jill all morning, gone to look for her in the afternoon and found her in the banyan tree. He had even dared the tarantulas to bring her back with him. She had neither reproached nor questioned him.

She had scarcely spoken to him. Now, at last, she spoke in a firm if wistful voice.

"I saw Curk try to kill you, Charlie. I was just at the edge of the beach when he flung you over the duff. You see, I had lingered to watch the sharks. They seemed so beautiful and peaceful when I swam with them. I thought they were my friends. Believe me, I didn't know what he meant to do. When you killed him, you and Gloomer were simply protecting yourselves."

"You mustn't think harshly of your father," Charlie said. He had never grown used to hearing her speak of "Curk" instead of "Father." "It's true he tried to sacrifice me. But I honestly believe that he felt he was sending me directly to his god. It was the greatest honor he could pay to an Englishman."

"I try to think of it that way. You see, I still love him, and I couldn't if I thought he was only cruel."

"Cruel isn't a word for a man like Curk. He didn't think in terms of good and bad, kind and cruel, but of strength and weakness."

"I know that, Charlie. And I was getting to be like him, wasn't I? But I like your way better now. You're strong and good. When we get to England, will I ever see you? Will you come down from Cambridge to see the girl who dressed like a pirate?"

"As often as I can!"

"I know you will as long as I'm with mother," she said without reproach. "You do love her, don't you?"

"Yes."

"I must pack now. All the gowns I never wore. I shall have to wear them in London. Do they still wear wigs at the balls?"

"Only the masquerades."

"On the voyage home, I will let my hair grow out. It grows fast and I should be presentable in a few months."

"You're more than presentable as you are. In a few months you'll be ravishing. The young men will flock around you like bees around a shower-of-gold tree."

"Do you know, I've never been farther than Martinique."

"You've a lot to see. But then, you've seen a lot, too. Right here on Oleandra."

"I could be content here, I think. I wouldn't miss the Caribs. Did you see how they turned away from me after Curk was dead? And how they carried their belongings down to the sea and loaded their dugouts and sailed away without even saying goodbye? They had only tolerated me because of Curk."

"He was their soul."

"Now they're soulless. They'll settle on another island and grow lazier and meaner, and get themselves killed off completely. And I did like them so much! I guess I saw them through Curk's eyes. As they had once been, in the old days. As they were at the festival, when Curk was praying to Tark. Charlie, will you excuse me? I don't want you to see me cry again."

She fled from the table and he sat alone in the forlorn, beautiful, beloved room where he had loved a woman and liked a girl, grieved for his mother and rejoiced in his friendship for me, Gloomer. He sat alone with the spirit of William Morris, with the oaken table and the red sideboard, and the tall, raftered ceiling.

He was lying in bed, his body a confusion of aches from his recent flight, his mind a confusion of thoughts in which the overriding thought was a question. Should he visit Elizabeth in the bedroom where she had secluded herself all day? He did not know if she were grieving for the death of Curk or rejoicing in her liberation; he did not know if she were waiting for him or avoiding him. The usually decisive Charlie felt himself inappropriately cast in the role of Hamlet instead of Childe Roland. Really, he thought, I have no right to intrude unless she sends for me. After all, when she wants someone she's rarely reticent. On the other hand, she may feel called on to mourn for the sake of appearances, when what she really wants is to, well, to visit with me.

"Master." It was Telesphorus, taper in hand, hovering in the door and looking as if he would flee should Charlie so much as raise his voice. He was not accustomed to disturbing English gentlemen, in their thoughts or in their sleep.

"Yes, Telesphorus. Have you a message for me?" The boy always looked so thin and woebegone that Charlie felt an urge to sit him down at a table and fatten him with partridges and puddings.

The thin little face brightened in the voluminous folds of his hood. His bare feet projected as usual from his robe, but looked as if they might be withdrawn as quickly as the feelers of a snail.

"The mistress says, will you come to her room, please?"

Charlie was already on his feet and lighting a taper from the one in Telesphorus' hands.

She had not only retired, she had drawn the curtains around her bed. The room lay in darkness except for Charlie's taper and a thin mist of moonlight.

"Put out the candle, my dear. I've been weeping, I'm afraid. I don't want you to see my bloodshot eyes." She squeezed his hand and drew him between the curtains, which fell into place with a silken rustle and closeted them in private night.

THE GOAT WITHOUT HORNS | 137

"Dearest Charlie, what horrors you've seen. And because of me."

He could scarcely see her in the dim light. She seemed not a woman but a disembodied spirit, and he felt like the knight forsaken on the cold hillside by La Belle Dame Sans Merci. There was not even a scent of frangipani to make her tangible.

Only when he took her in his arms did he feel assured of her presence. "Elizabeth, it's you who have seen the horrors. For fifteen years. A man like Curk—"

"A man? I know what he was, my dear. You were right to keep the truth from Jill. But I can guess what really happened. How he came after you, and not as a man. And how he died in combat with Gloomer. I've suspected the truth for years. There are Carib folktales about such beings. But I told myself they were cruel, stupid myths. How could I live with such a one and know the truth about him?"

"Is it over now; the horror, I mean? Is Jill really free of him? I don't mean of loving him—after all, he was her father—but of becoming like him?" Charlie asked.

"She was never in danger herself. Only the males are so afflicted, or honored, in the eyes of the Caribs. That was the reason Curk wanted me to bear him a son. When I failed, he wanted a grandson."

"And if Jill should marry in England and have a son?"

"She can bear a dozen sons without danger of perpetuating the...affliction. Only had she been with child—a male child—when she swam with the sharks would there have been a danger. You see, the ritual was more than prayers and torchlight. It was actually meant to be a transformation of the unborn child. I know as much from the folktales. And because I myself once swam with the sharks, except that I loathed and feared them, while Jill adores them, or did, until they threatened you. That was before I took to my bed. That was why I took to my bed. And because of Curk's rage when I bore him a daughter. Had I born him a son—"

"He would have been like Curk?"

"Yes."

Charlie shook his head. "No one would believe us in England, or even in Martinique. There's nothing in Darwin's science to account for such beings. He writes of evolution. This is devolution."

"Nonetheless, they are very real. There were similar beings in Europe before the Church destroyed them. We called them werewolves. Darwin is right, I think, that men evolved from the beasts, but from many beasts—wolves, bears, sharks—and not just apes. In Curk's case, we have both the evolving man and the ancestral beast in the same person."

He held her with a wild tenderness. "Don't talk about him any more. Leave him where he belongs. In the past. In the world's past."

She made a faint pretense of pushing him away from her, but quickly yielded to his insistent arms. "Charlie, I am fifty years old. You are nineteen. Here, we can love each other and no one will ridicule us. In England, we would be ridiculous. Like a French couple. One of those aging literary ladies like George Sand with her young lover."

"Then we'll stay here. But you don't look aging, you look blooming! And I can grow a mustache and look at least twenty-five. No one would say a thing except how lucky I was to win such a beautiful bride."

"My beauty is very important to you, isn't it, my dear?"

"I love your proud, gallant soul. But I love your beauty too. How can I reach your soul except through your body?"

"Keats said much the same thing to Fanny Brawne, and both of you are right, of course. *'Why may I not speak of your Beauty, since without that I could never have loved you. I cannot conceive any beginning of such love as I have for you but Beauty.'*"

Charlie continued the letter without a pause. " *'There may be a sort of love for which, without the least sneer at it, I have the highest respect and can admit it in others; but it has not the richness, the bloom, the full form, the enchantment of love after my own heart.'"*

"You knew it, by heart, of course. I knew that you would. It's impossible for young men to love any other way, and I must confess that your own kind soul would not have stirred me so much if you had looked like Telesphorus' father instead of your golden self. But blooming or not, I can't stay on Oleandra with you now. Jill must return to England for an education and eventually a marriage."

"Can't I still tutor her on Oleandra? That was the reason you brought me here."

"It's a little awkward when mother and daughter are in love with the same young man. And I myself have English yearnings for the opera, the theatre, the ballroom. The Season in London and the Season at Bath. Icicles under the eaves. Daffodils bringing the spring. 'O to be in England now that April's there…'"

"Then I'm going with you, and I promise to pester you until you become my bride!"

"Your bride? Charlie, you're still a moralist at heart, aren't you? You want to make me an honest woman. I'm deeply touched. But hearth fires don't become me. Neither does arguing, my dear. Stay with me tonight. Tomorrow you may change your mind about several things."

He was awakened by the chirping of sugar birds among the morning glories. He opened the curtains to the bed and walked to the window. The diminutive birds, like winged daffodils, flickered among the blossoms and shook the dew from the petals into miniken showers.

"Elizabeth, wake up! The birds have come back. And you have your daffodils!"

She stirred toward wakefulness. A sunbeam fell on her face. He gasped and she opened her eyes.

"I'm sorry, my dear. I can see that you see. I wish it were otherwise. I wish I were what you loved."

She was still beautiful as a woman of fifty; she would have challenged a Michelangelo to capture the complexity of character, the variety of experience in the lines of her forehead and the wrinkles around her eyes. She was a woman who had sometimes been bitter and sometimes unfaithful, sometimes happy and usually kind; an unloving wife but a loving if not always wise mother. He was not frightened of her, but he was frightened for her. On this island of dark miracles, shock and grief, he supposed, had aged her in two nights.

She drew him beside her and touched his cheek with moth-light fingers. "Don't be sad. I wanted you to see me like this. This is the way I am. The beauty you loved was an illusion. You once called me the Lady of the Frangipanis. I am such a lady in a very literal sense. When Curk first came to me—it was my first visit to his island—he brought me a tiny vial of transparent blue elixir like a draught from the sea above a coral reef in the morning sun.

"'The Spaniards looked for a fountain of youth,' he said. 'It was all around them and they never even saw it. It was in the nectar of the flowers they trampled under their boots. Frangipani and shower-of-gold and…but the rest is my secret. How old do you think I am?'

"'Thirty-five? Forty? There are no guides in your face. Not the least wrinkled. Only your eyes look somehow…very old,' I told him.

"'I am seventy-four,' he answered. 'Would you like to look always as you do now? I can't promise you immortality—you will live perhaps to a hundred. But your skin will maintain the illusion of youth until you die. One drop a day, and time will be your friend.'

"'And what do you ask in return?'

"'I want to make love to an English woman and I want her to bear my child.'

"Thus I was bound to him, Charlie, in spite of his cruelties, and also because I loved him. He could have had me without any gift of youth, but he thought that he had to buy me. He thought of English women as high and proud, a race of conquerors and colonizers who looked upon Caribs, even their kings, as savages who needed to be civilized. Later I could have escaped my desire for him, but not my wish to be desirable. Charlie, I love all beautiful things. A sonnet by Mrs. Browning. A tapestry woven by William Morris. I can't be wrinkled and old and forgotten. Do you understand?"

"Of course I do," he faltered, as pity warred with desire. "But old things are usually best."

"Only on a shelf with other old things."

"But I don't love you for your face, Elizabeth!"

"You love me for my soul? Perhaps. But you have to look through my face to see my soul. You yourself have said as much. I don't say that you must love me less now. But differently. Look upon me as one who understood your grief for your mother and almost but not quite managed to fill her place."

He took her in his arms and she held him with a last wild yearning.

"Goodbye, my dear, goodbye. We shall never meet again like this, but I do love you, Charlie."

They stood in the rocky enclave facing the sea, where Charlie had landed one month, one love, ago. Charlie, Elizabeth, and Jill; the old man and Telesphorus tethering the donkeys to outcroppings of rock. Except for Telesphorus and his father, who would stay on the island and care for the house, they were going back to England. Charlie was going back to Cambridge. (Oh, my friend, how may I follow you to those icy northern seas? Look in the wake of whatever ship you board, and I will begin the journey to bring you luck, but England is far and her seas are bleak, in spite of the Gulf Stream's warmth.)

The sailors were rowing manfully and swearing whenever a wave broke across their bow, and no doubt wondering what had happened to those shifty Caribs whose one skill and one duty was coming to meet the schooner.

Charlie was alternately waving encouragement to them and trying to coax Elizabeth to take a seat on a rock which he had brushed clean for her at the cost of ruining his handkerchief, a bright blue square of silk which was now diminished to brown.

"You must sit down and rest," he urged. "You know how it tires you to ride a burro."

"I'm too excited to sit." Brilliant as bougainvillea in a gown of many colors, she was smiling and waving to the men in the boat and looking as if she never went to bed until morning, and not at all when she could dance or play chemin-de-fer. Not only had she partaken generously of her elixir—two drops instead of one—and repaired the ravages of her brief abstinence, she had sent Telesphorus to search Curk's house, and the staunch little fellow, rooting through the loft, had returned with several precious flagons, a supply for many years, which Elizabeth promptly designated 'My special wine—nobody else likes it.'

In such a sea, on such a precipitous island, a longboat could not land; she could merely hover and try not to crash. The stalwart if simian rowers, at the expense of three broken oars and uncountable twisted muscles, somehow managed to hold her off the rocks. Their oaths turned to cries of delight when they recognized Elizabeth, the mysterious lady of Frangipanis come to welcome them or rather, to judge by her trunks, come to return with them to Martinique.

Boarding the boat would have been worse than a problem, it would have been an impossibility for Elizabeth had she remained a bedridden invalid. But when a lusty young seaman held out his arms to her, she made the considerable leap across several frothing feet of water to land and linger within his harboring arms. Jill, of course, had no difficulty. With the grace of a flying fish, she jumped and landed to the cheers though not the embraces of the sailors. Once Charlie had followed her (as yet he was lingering on the island), the rowers would deposit them aboard the schooner and then return for their trunks, small ones in view of the traveling conditions, which would somehow be handed or heaved from shore (and hopefully not spilled) by Telesphorus and his father.

The old man was red-eyed and Telesphorus was openly bawling at the loss of their beloved mistress.

"Good-bye, my dears," Elizabeth called. "Keep the house ready for Jill and me, and we'll come back to you, we promise." Then, as a seeming afterthought, "And mind you load my 'special wine' carefully. Davy Jones doesn't need it, and neither do the sharks!"

All this time Charlie had lingered on the shore, though by now the sailors were swearing at him like the Caribs on his arrival. He knelt on a rock, leaned over the water, and gave me a parting pat even while foam from the surf splattered his face. He did not know that I intended to follow him to England (hoped to, I should say). He would never have allowed me to attempt so dangerous a trip.

"Gloomer," he said. "I'm coming back one day. Will you still be in our lagoon?"

"Gnu." How could I stay in the lagoon and also follow him to England?

"What's that you say?" he cried.

To ease his mind, I told him my first falsehood. "Iss.

"Goodbye, old friend. Best friend." His face was wet and not with the spray. Humans have one advantage over dolphins. We have no tears to ease us out of our sadness and we seem to be smiling even when we are saddest.

I swam under him as he jumped aboard the boat, and frolicked around the boat as it battled toward the schooner. I spun in the air, made those clicking noises which humans suppose to be laughter, and all in all attempted to tease my friend from his melancholy (and forget the tears I could not shed). But he looked at me with a wan, sorrowful smile; not at the island, not at the schooner, not even at the newly radiant Elizabeth, but at me, always at me, and his look was enough to break my heart.

They were almost at the schooner now. The friendly captain was booming a welcome. Seeing Elizabeth among his passengers, he straightened his cap and jacket, smoothed his whiskers, and strode to the gunwale to receive her aboard his ship.

"Elizabeth," Charlie said. "Can you use a caretaker for the Red House? If you had a dependable one, you would never need to sell it. He would keep it up so well that you would want to come back for sure, at least for a visit now and then."

"Charlie, do you really want to stay?"

"I'm afraid Gloomer will try to follow me all the way to England. He would never be happy in those cold northern waters. Besides, I love the house. You're coming back. You said so yourself."

"So am I," said Jill. "After I've grown a bosom and learned some wiles from mother."

"You're fine as you are." He gave her a wet, brotherly kiss on the cheek.

"Your kiss says I'm not. But I shall expect a different kind when you see me again."

"Stay, then, Charlie," said Elizabeth, oblivious to the rowers, who were more intent on this curious domestic drama than they were on reaching their ship. "I'll miss you, though, in England. One's first love is very precious, and I am honored to have been your first. Equally precious is one's last love, and that is what you are to me."

He seized her hand and held it against his cheek. "You won't be lonely in London?"

Charlie, Charlie, I wanted to cry. Do you really think this beautiful, sentimental, and mischievous lady will ever be lonely in London or anywhere else, or want for young men to pay her court? It was well that I said nothing, or that, had I spoken, I would not have been understood. In a way, I was unfair to her. She really believed that Charlie was her last love. Whatever she said, she believed at the time; it was just that she sometimes changed her mind.

He was already removing his clothes. Shoes, middy jacket, and bell-bottom trousers, but not, fortunately, his under garments.

"Forgive me, Elizabeth and Jill. But I can't swim to shore with all this clutter."

The rowers had almost stopped rowing.

"What's the lad doin'?"

"Strippin" for a swim, I reckon."

"Before the ladies? Blimey, 'e's no gentleman. E's one of us!"

Then he was in the water, waving over his shoulder and calling a last goodbye to his departing friends, and turning to meet and greet me with a radiant, "Hello, Gloomer, I've come back. I told you I would, didn't I?"

"Isss."

A big wave almost inundated him. I dove under him and he clasped my dorsal fin and we swam for the island and the passage and our own green lagoon.

Made in the USA
Charleston, SC
05 September 2013